'He seems like a nice boy,' she said, about two weeks after I started seeing him. 'But if he messes you about I'll cut off his danglies with a pair of garden shears.'

'It's not him I need to worry about, Nat,' I told her.

'You on about your family?'

I nodded at her. 'Yeah. I'm going to have to be ultra-secretive. They'll kill me if I get found out.'

'Not with me around, babe. They'll have to kill me first.'

Critical acclaim for *(un)arranged marriage*:
'Absorbing and engaging . . . unusual because it is written from a male point of view . . . a highly readable debut from Bali Rai that teenagers of any culture will identify with'
Observer

'Energetically and pacily written . . . There is a vitality and freshness about Rai's writing that engages the reader . . . An intriguing debut that promises well for the future'
Books for Keeps

Critical acclaim for *The Crew*:
'Written in a streetwise dialect, this is a jewel of a book'
Independent

'Engagingly direct in tone, grittily realistic in theme, this uncompromising, streetwise story is sure to appeal'
Books for Keeps

Also available by Bali Rai,
and published by Corgi Books:

(un)arranged marriage
The Crew

RANI & SUKH

bali rai

corgi books

RANI & SUKH
A CORGI BOOK : 9780552548908

First published in Great Britain by Corgi Books,
an imprint of Random House Children's Books

Corgi edition published 2004

13 15 17 19 20 18 16 14

The Random House Group Limited supports The Forest Stewardship Council
(FSC®), the leading international forest certification organisation. Our books
carrying the FSC label are printed on FSC® certified paper. FSC is the only
forest certification scheme endorsed by the leading environmental organisations,
including Greenpeace. Our paper procurement policy can be found at
www.randomhouse.co.uk/environment

Set in Bembo MT Schoolbook 12/14.5pt
by Falcon Oast Graphic Art Ltd.

Corgi Books are published by Random House Children's Books,
61–63 Uxbridge Road, London W5 5SA,
A Random House Group Company

Addresses for companies within The Random House Group Limited
can be found at:
www.randomhouse.co.uk/offices.htm

THE RANDOM HOUSE GROUP Limited Reg. No. 954009
www.kidsatrandomhouse.co.uk

A CIP catalogue record for this book is available from the British Library.

Printed and bound by
CPI Group (UK) Ltd, Croydon, CR0 4YY

MIX
Paper from
responsible sources
FSC
www.fsc.org   FSC® C016897

Thank you to all the usual suspects, Penny, Jennifer;
and to Gooch, Bind and Divy Heer
for all the parents' evenings and stuff
(and for calling me Professor Balthazar!).

I wouldn't have been able to write this book without
the support, input and love of Jasmine Powdrill,
to whom I'd like to dedicate it.
You will wear suntan lotion . . . Love you. XXX

BEGINNING . . .

The moon gave off a silvery haze, barely highlighting the path ahead. Towards the north, the track led down to the centre of the village, leading into narrow lanes and gullies of one- and two-storey dwellings daubed in lime and fuchsia, with vines and creepers edging their green fingers across the walls. To the south lay open fields, rice paddies sweltering in the heat, long-standing grasses and ears of corn swathed in darkness; and freedom.

She stood for a moment and tried to get her bearings. Screams rang through her head. Screams and then laughter, one following the other. Accusations and exclamations. Memories flashed by. Her beloved. The muscles that rippled through his skin, the soft golden-brown hairs that covered his chest. She shivered as she recalled his gentle caress. His creamy clouded skin, so soft, so different from that of any other man she had ever seen. Hazel eyes that shone and sparkled with the promise of love. For ever . . .

She shuddered and moved on, heading south, fearful that her father was behind her. Maybe her brothers too – with their crimson-covered hands, cudgels swinging. She moved quickly despite the darkness, every step taken from memory – years of walking this same way, to take *roti* and *dhal* out to her father and her brothers as they toiled in the heat of the midday sun, ploughing and planting and tending and harvesting. Late-night trips before bed time that eventually became clandestine meetings with him . . .

Now, as she fled the wrath of her family, she recalled nothing of the warmth and love and joy that had formed her fifteen years on Earth. She felt only anger and fear. And deep inside, as some invisible hand forced her on, nestled just above the forming head of her unborn child, she felt a stabbing, cloying pain which threatened to sap the strength from her bones and the will from her heart. But she pushed on and on. And on . . .

The well sat alone in the middle of a disused square of land, surrounded on all sides by tall grasses and hemp plants. The stone from which it had been built three hundred years earlier appeared shiny and almost metallic under the moonlight. Everything round about sat in utter darkness yet the well stood out, as if it were an omen. She stood barely five paces from it, searching the night sky. Tears coursed their way down her cheeks as she tried and tried to make sense of what had happened. Why it had happened.

'*Das Menhu,*' she implored her maker. 'Tell me why . . . ?'

She noticed a bright star, directly above her. Above the well. It was him. She knew it. Already he was waiting, just as he had always promised, in those stolen moments among the long ears of corn, and out here at the very spot where she stood.

'If I go before you,' he'd whispered to her, caressing her soft, naked belly, 'then I will wait for you. Up there, in the sky.'

'How will I find you, *meri jaan*?' she'd replied.

He'd smiled, his eyes sparkling. 'You will find me up there, at night. The brightest of all the stars. Waiting for you.'

'But we have our whole lives ahead of us.'

'*Tu heh, meri jaan,*' he'd told her, kissing her gently on the lips.

Now she repeated his words to herself. *You are my life. You are my life . . .*

And there he was, just as he had promised, above her head. High up in the Heavens. Awaiting her. She paused and considered how fate had played such a cruel trick on her, taking her heart away and leaving only a trace of him inside her. She held her belly and cried for her child. She looked up again, shedding more tears, an unstoppable flow now. He was still waiting.

Meri jaan.

She edged towards the well, sat on the wall and waited another moment or two. Long enough to tell her child that she loved it. Long enough to tell her beloved that she was on her way. Long enough to try and make recompense with her maker.

'*Meri maafi kaaro-ji*,' she cried. 'Forgive me, my Lord.'

And then she fell . . .

LEICESTER

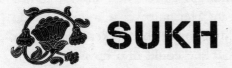 # SUKH

'Man, she's wicked. Like one of them Bollywood actresses. Fine.'

Sukh was sitting on the steps that led up to the concrete tennis courts by the side of school, talking to one of his friends, Jaspal.

Jaspal laughed and shook his head. 'Rani? You know what her name means, don't you?'

'Yeah – it means "queen", don't it?'

'Exactly, Sukh. Queen. She probably loves herself, you get me?'

'How can you say that when you don't even know her, man?'

Sukh shook his head and looked at Jas. What an arse. The boy didn't even get the *nasty* girls in school checkin' for him, never mind the fittest girl *smiling* – like she had at Sukh. Rani Sandhu. The wickedest girl in school. Smiling. At him. He couldn't help it. He grinned to himself.

Rani Sandhu was the most beautiful girl he had ever seen. She had soft, creamy skin and hazel eyes flecked with green splinters, full of light and life. Her mouth

9

was full, with beautiful lips that he had an urge to kiss whenever he saw them. Her hair was a honeyed shade of brown, straight and long. She looked just like a Bollywood actress but she could also have passed for a Spanish girl. Or an Italian. She was the perfect height for Sukh, just a little shorter than him, with a voluptuous figure – the kind of look he loved.

'You're just jealous, Jas,' said Sukh. 'That green-eyed monster catch a hold of you.'

'Sack that,' laughed Jaspal. 'She's OK. Wouldn't say she was anything special though.'

Jas eyed a couple of girls walking by, one of them white, the other Asian, as his friend continued to bait him. 'Yeah, I know you wouldn't. The only girls smile at you are in *Asian Babes*. You know – naked and flat.'

Sukh ducked the friendly punch that Jas threw his way, laughing at his own joke. Jas got up from the step and dusted off his D & G jeans, copied from the original cut at his father's clothing factory. He looked down at Sukh.

'Enoughing of ju shit, Sukhbinderjit,' he said, in a piss-take of his dad's Anglo-Asian accent.

'Jealous?' challenged Sukh.

'Yeah, yeah. If you is so bad why don't you go and chat to her? Get her digits for your phone?' replied Jaspal.

'What? And transport her to a flower garden in Kashmir, yeah? Like in them Bollywood films you love like they is your girlfriend?'

'Piss off, man,' answered Jas, looking embarrassed.

'I can see it now. I walk over and smile at her as she's standing giggling with her friends. She swoons and falls at my feet. Lies there for a second, panting and then – *boom!* – we're in that garden, dancing round the roses, making eyes at each other, blowing kisses, while some old bag wails in Hindi and a thousand dancers appear from nowhere – and then the kiss . . . Yeah, I can see it now. She hides behind a tree and I try to find her, but she moves from tree to tree like something that . . . er . . . *moves* a lot, and then I catch her and just as we kiss the camera cuts to a shot of the bees landing on the flowers—'

'You fool,' replied Jas, laughing.

'Better a fool than a wanker, Jas. Believe that.'

Sukh ducked another punch before getting up and following Jas back into school for an afternoon of GCSE English and maths and thoughts of Rani Sandhu.

# RANI

I was sitting in my English lit. classroom waiting for the rest of my group to get there. I was practising my reading of Shakespeare so that I wouldn't mess it up if I got asked to read out loud. Not like my best friend Nat, who had made the whole class laugh in the last lesson by fluffing her lines and then re-reading her passage in a Latino accent, like some Mexican actress. The thing was, I couldn't concentrate on the book. It was the last thing on my mind. I was thinking about that boy, Sukh, who I kept smiling at for no reason at all. If I saw him walking down the corridor I'd break out in a smile like some silly little girl. It was embarrassing. But I couldn't help myself. It happened every time I saw him. He was so fit.

I was smiling to myself when Nat walked into the classroom, swung her bag off her shoulder and slammed it down on the table in front of me.

'*Nat!* Bloody hell, you made me jump,' I said.

'Relax, babe – I was only putting my bag down. You'd think I had shot you or something.'

'Have you practised reading the text this time?' I

asked, after my heart had stopped trying to jump out of my mouth.

'Oh *yeah* – 'cos I haven't got anything better to do with my evenings than sit around reading William,' she replied.

I laughed. 'So that means you haven't?'

Nat shrugged. 'Dev came round so I had other things on my mind. Like *his* William . . .' She grinned at me like a cat.

'*Natalie!* I can't believe you just said that – get thee to a nunnery!'

'Oh, *chill out* – I'm kidding,' replied Nat, smiling.

I decided to change the subject. 'I got that *Bend It Like Beckham* out last night—' I began.

'Tell you what – that Beckham – man, oh man, would he—'

'I don't want to hear it, Nat. Seriously, I'm getting worried about you and your hormones. Isn't it boys who are supposed to be like dogs in heat at this age?'

'Equal rights, sister. I can say and do what I like,' replied Nat, smiling. 'And anyway, I saw the way you were smiling to yourself when I walked in. Like some demented nun high on ecstasy.'

'I was not!'

'Yeah you were – thinking 'bout that Sukh again?'

I smiled at her. Well, what else was I supposed to do? 'Maybe . . .' I said coyly, for maximum dramatic effect.

'Rani – you little minx, you!' laughed Nat, looking surprised at me.

'He's lovely,' I replied, smiling even wider.

Nat shook her head, walking around to the other side of the table to sit down. The rest of the class were beginning to file in slowly. She lowered her voice. 'Why don't you ask him out?' she said.

'I can't – my family ain't exactly the most liberated people . . .'

'What they don't know won't give them a coronary, will it?' answered Nat in a whisper, an allowance for the fact that the teacher, Miss Crumb, had walked in and was asking for silence.

'Maybe,' I said, turning my attention to the lesson.

Behind me someone said something about someone else's feet being smelly.

'Quiet!' Miss Crumb shushed them and turned to Nat. 'Natalie – can you read from Act Three, Scene Five, please?'

'Me?' asked Nat, pointing to herself. 'Why, gladly I will, miss. In this day and age, with children more interested in computer games and ruining the English language with T-X-T M-S-G-S, it must be a real comfort to know that you have such a *dedicated* pupil as me. A real *crumb* of comfort . . .'

The classroom erupted with laughter as Miss Crumb mock applauded. 'Yes – very clever, Natalie . . .'

I just smiled again, and then all I could think about was Sukh Bains . . .

 **RANI**

My name means 'queen' in Punjabi, the language of my parents. Sometimes it's a name that I don't mind and occasionally it's like a noose around my neck — especially when the other Punjabi kids at school latch onto it. Even my best mate Natalie rips me over it. Calls me *Bollywood ki Rani*. Bollywood Queen.

The thing about names is that they all mean something. And sometimes they can get you into trouble . . .

Sukh finally plucked up the courage to talk to me about a week after we first noticed each other. We'd come up from primary to secondary school at the same time and not spoken in the years since. Which, if you think about it, is quite weird. It took Natalie to make a remark about how sexy Sukh's bum looked in jeans to get me to notice him. Generally the lads at school are either minging or stupid. Most of them are still babies really. They crowd around porn magazines in gangs and giggle at the naked women, or they fight because one of them looked at the other the 'wrong way'. Stupid little kids with spots, greasy hair and no concept of hormonal control. Not to mention BO and smelly feet. Nasty.

The first time I looked at him properly my heart skipped a beat. No – seriously. I know it sounds all stupid and that, but it honestly did. I looked at him and he looked back, right into my eyes, and I started to blush and feel hot all over. Talk about fit. His eyes were this beautiful amber-brown colour, like pools that you could jump into and swim in. Pools of honey. And when he smiled he just looked so beautiful, with those big eyes and really thick, long lashes, just like a girl's; and his soft, coffee-coloured skin, totally kissable lips and white teeth that sparkled . . .

Nat pissed herself laughing when I told her all of that. She started singing a song from an India Arie CD, called 'Brown Skin', and what made it worse was that Nat has a voice like an angel, so I couldn't even diss her back over her singing. She's so talented. Sings, dances, acts. She's five foot eight, with a body most girls would die for. You know – great tits, perfect bum. Long legs. Long brown hair. Lips like Angelina Jolie. The lucky cow. She should be on the next *Pop Idol* thing on the telly. Then again, maybe she has too much talent for that.

I walked off in embarrassment that first time I saw Sukh and then I had to wait a whole week before he finally got the message and came over to ask me out. Nat had spent all that time trying to let him know that I liked him via his stupid mate Jaspal. It was hard going. Jaspal wanted to make up a foursome with Natalie, who already has a boyfriend – Dev – and when she made it clear that she found him about as attractive as a rancid dishcloth, Jas refused to talk to Sukh for me. But Nat had other plans up her sleeve. She followed Sukh around all week, popping up everywhere he went, just in case he wanted to ask her about me – the lunch queue, the bus stop. She even went into the boys' changing rooms at one point.

'You went *into* the boys' locker room?' I asked her, ashamed of the brazen hussy who was my best friend. Ashamed and strangely proud too.

'Yeah – it's no big deal,' she said. 'He wasn't there anyway, and besides they were all dressed. Talk about anticlimax, babe.'

'I should hope so,' I replied, smiling. I looked at Nat.

'OK,' she said, 'back to the real mission. No, I didn't speak to him. I think he's scared of me, Rani. Honestly.'

I gave her a quizzing look. '*Scared? Of you*? Surely not.'

The sarcasm registered. 'Very funny,' replied Nat, putting on a hurt look.

'Oh pack it in, Nat. I'm not your mum.'

She broke out in a grin. 'You look old enough to be,' she said.

'You cheeky little— Look, I'm not interested in petty jibes, girl. What am I gonna do about Sukh?'

'You could try just going up to him and asking him out,' suggested Nat.

'*Me?* Ask *him?* Sod that. I'm a romantic at heart. None of your bra-burning liberation for me, m'dear.'

'Equality, sister,' laughed Nat. 'You're either with us or against us.'

I sighed. 'Oh, the *stupid* little boy. What am I gonna do?'

Eventually Natalie just walked right up to Sukh while he was standing in the dinner queue, grabbed him by the arm and told him that if he came quietly she wouldn't be forced to bite him where it hurts, right there in front of everyone. Funnily enough he followed her. I was in the library, entertaining the other side of my split personality, the snotty swot kid from the land of Geek who always did her homework on time, when in stormed Natalie with Sukh in tow.

'Right,' she said, pointing at me. 'This is my friend Rani. She's fit and she's clever and if I was a lad *I'd* give her one and she fancies you – you lucky little man . . .'

Sukh went a shade of red that only Asians can. He was looking at anyone, anything, but me. And especially not at Nat, who hadn't finished yet.

'And I don't care about all that my-parents-don't-want-me-to-go-out-with-girls crap. Just lie to them. Everyone else does . . .'

Sukh frowned. 'But my parents don't give a shit who I—' he began.

'Don't be rude, Sukh – Mummy's speaking,' snapped

Natalie, cutting him short. Talk about shut him up. He just looked down at his feet.

'So be a good boy and ask her out, will you?' finished Nat, finally taking a breather.

I looked at him and grinned. My cutest, I-know-this-look-gets-the-men-going face. And then something in my head went *pop* and my heart skipped a beat. Like magic or something.

'Hi,' he said, through the haze of dreamy thoughts that flooded through my mind.

'Hi,' I replied, smiling.

'Erm . . . do you . . . er . . . fancy—?'

'Yeah she does,' said Natalie, answering for me. 'Meet her after school – down by the gates.'

Sukh looked from me to Nat and then back at me, smiling wide. 'OK,' he said to me. 'See you later, Rani.' He turned and walked out of the library.

'My, oh *my*, his ass looks fine in them jeans,' sighed Nat, watching him go.

'He said my *name*,' I told her with an inane grin. '*He* said *my* name.'

Natalie looked at me with something approaching pity. 'Oh my God . . .' she said, shaking her head.

We met, Sukh and me, out by the gates after school and he walked me to the bus stop. Well actually, he walked me *and* Natalie to the bus stop, but Nat did keep a discreet distance behind us. Like all of two feet. Still, it was so nice just to talk to him and realize that he was promising. He didn't giggle once, made no reference to his favourite football team and said nothing about collecting things of any kind. And he smelled nice – clean and fresh, which is always a must. By the time we arrived at the bus stop I was already in love. Well, you know what I mean . . . There was just something about him that made me smile inside. Because we were both from British Punjabi families I asked him what his surname was.

He smiled at me. 'Bains,' he said.

'Mine's Sandhu,' I said.

I asked him what his star sign was.

'Sagittarius – my birthday's on the first of December.'

As my bus pulled into the stop I nearly fell over. 'December the *first*?' I repeated.

Sukh gave me a funny look. 'Yeah – why?'

I stepped onto the bus. 'It's the same day as mine,' I told him. He started to speak but I put my finger to my lips. 'See you tomorrow.'

I watched him as the bus moved away until he disappeared out of sight.

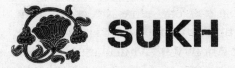 # SUKH

Sukh stood and watched the bus disappear into the distance, feeling himself shiver slightly. There was something about Rani Sandhu that made him feel possessed. He felt drawn to her. And not just because he fancied her like crazy. There was something else. The way she looked at him. The little lights that flickered in her eyes. The way she held her head when she spoke to him. The soft, musical tone of her voice. It was like he already knew her – knew what she was going to say and how she would say it. When she looked at him it felt as though his face were being bathed in a warm light. And inside him something other than raging hormones stirred – something that he could never talk to his mates about. And then there was the business about sharing a birthday. Was that Rani having a laugh or was it true? Did they really share their birthday? How weird would that be if it were true?

He shook his head and turned back towards the school. He had football practice and was late. Hopefully Jaspal had covered for him. He thought about the upcoming City Cup Final between his school and a less racially mixed school from an estate out to the east of the city. The game was going to be hard. Hard and dirty. The estate wasn't known as the kind of place where Asians were particularly welcome. And their school team was good. He wondered who the coach would pick for the side, but the closer he got to the school gates, the more his thoughts drifted back to the events of earlier in the day.

There was the good-looking mad girl who was Rani's best friend, Natalie – the kind of girl that scared most of the lads because she was so upfront and straight about things like sex. Most of the boys in Sukh's year called her a slag and that, but in a strange way Sukh actually admired her. She was independent and didn't take any crap from them. She reminded Sukh of his own sister, although Parvy was much older and lived on her own; she worked for a big recruitment agency. Sukh's family had wanted Parvy to get married in the traditional way, to a boy from the right caste and culture and all that, but Parvy had just packed up and left.

Sukh was proud of his sister. She wasn't some timid, shrinking-violet type like lots of other Asian women, who bowed to the pressure from their families. She was a go-getter and Sukh liked that. She also had a wicked flat in a converted hosiery mill in the centre of Leicester, which was empty because Parvy was away, working for her company in New York. And she had given Sukh a key. What was not to like?

The reaction to Parvy leaving hadn't been like a bomb going off. Sukh's father, Resham Bains, hadn't threatened suicide, murder and every combination in between. He hadn't threatened to kill Parvy, kill her mother, kill himself. Gas the entire family. Not like in a lot of traditional Punjabi families, where Parvy's actions would have been seen to dishonour the family name. Instead he had gone into a sulk that lasted for all of a month before Sukh's mum had put her husband straight. He was just angry that Parvy had won a power struggle against him – and become 'the bloody fish 'n' chip *goreeh*', as Sukh's dad put it. Become a Westerner. Sukh's mum had pointed out that their daughter was an educated woman and had the right to pursue her career, regardless of tradition. Sukh had agreed with his mum. What had his old man expected, asking them to grow up in England? Not to become English?

Sukh's elder brother, Ravinder, had toed the line of tradition without being asked and married some girl from Birmingham, all arranged by the family. He lived on the other side of Leicester with his wife Kamal, but was always coming round to see their mum. As for Sukh – well, he was far too young to even consider stuff like weddings but he knew one thing for sure – whoever he eventually married, it was going to be for love and not out of some stupid desire to uphold honour or tradition.

Parvy still got a load of grief from the rest of their

extended family – from every uncle and cousin, and every unrelated fat bastard who came from the same village in India and had moved to Leicester. They all had something to say. Sukh winced as he remembered punching one of his cousins, Daljit, because he'd said that Parvy would end up on the street, like a prostitute, without the support of her family. Sukh remembered how angry he'd become – he wasn't about to let anyone slag off his sister, family or not.

And then there was Rani herself.

Even thinking about her gave Sukh butterflies. As he made his way towards the locker rooms he thought about her face, her hair, the way her hips swayed when she walked. The proud way her breasts sat in her shirt. And then he shook his head as if he were trying to shake such thoughts out of himself. He was going to have to hide what he was thinking from the lads – imagine the grief they'd give him if he went all chick-flick on *them*?

Try as he did, though, he just couldn't stop thinking about her. Not even halfway through the practice session when he needed to concentrate on marking his opponent. Not when he missed the ball completely two metres from the goal line. And not even when he was in the showers surrounded by his mates, all laughing and joking and chatting pure slackness about the girls they had dealt with – mostly in their dreams. Man, he had the bug and he had it *bad*.

But there was something worrying his blissful

thoughts too, nagging at the heart of his new-found heaven, only he couldn't work out what exactly. Some kind of vague memory that he didn't want to be bothered by. Instead he missed the bus on purpose and walked home on a cloud, singing some lover's rock tune in his head, something that Parvy listened to all the time.

 **RANI**

I started seeing Sukh properly after that first walk to the bus stop. Well, when I say properly, I mean as my actual boyfriend. I'd had male friends before – you know, the kind of guys you flirt with at school, generally ones in the years above, who seem so much easier to talk to and more interesting than the geeks who are the same age as you. But I'd never actually had a boyfriend. Not a real, actual, call-up-all-the-time and text-till-your-fingers-ache kind of boy. I was excited and nervous and a bit scared all at the same time. I mean, what if I was wrong about him and he was just like all the other boys in my year? The kind that tells his mates everything that he does with his girlfriend. And I'm not talking about shopping either . . . I'd seen boys like that, talking about which bits of their girlfriend they had touched or seen naked and all that immature stuff. Real bastards who were just using the girls they were with. Like the guy Natalie lost her virginity to.

He was called Martin and he was in the year above us. Nat had pursued him for ages. She really fancied him and I suppose he was kind of nice, in a rugby player sort of way – if you like that sort of thing. He was all shoulders, thighs, big smile – and hairy arse, according to Nat. And eventually he'd given in and gone out with her. First it was all about holding hands and five text messages a day, and then dates to the cinema and shopping trips to Nottingham and stuff. Nat was really happy and I was really pleased for her because she was smiling all the time and seemed to have found the right man.

And then he started telling her that he loved her and that he wanted to stay with her for ever – real Hollywood romance type things. Nat, for all her bravado and independent-woman crap, is a hopeless romantic at heart. She took Martin seriously when he told her that he wanted to sleep with her, to take their relationship on to the next level, as he put it. Eventually, at some house party thrown by one of Martin's friends that I hadn't been allowed to go to, Nat slept with him. I couldn't believe it when she told me about it the next day. I mean, she was only four-teen – it was against the law. And I had all these moral arguments going on too, burned into my conscience by my family. No sex before marriage. No boyfriends before marriage. Let's face it, as far as my family were concerned, with me it was no *nothing* before marriage. That's why I had been so shocked – it was just some-thing that I thought I'd never do, not unless I was really in love.

But Nat *was* really into him and she believed him when he said that he felt the same. Then, the following Monday at school, he just blanked her. Like she didn't exist. Stopped sending her texts, ignored her when she passed him in the corridor. Serious, big-time wanker type stuff.

Nat was distraught. She felt used and dirty, and no matter how much I tried to tell her differently, she thought that everyone at school was talking about her – so much so that at one point she didn't come to school for a week. It was really horrible seeing my best friend go through so much pain and anguish. Some of the other girls at school made it even worse by calling her a slag and calling me names too, just for defending her. One gang of Asian girls were really nasty. They went and spread rumours all over school about how Nat would sleep with anyone. It was horrible.

That's why Nat ended up seeing Dev. Not only because he was genuinely nice but because he didn't go to our school and he waited for nearly six months before he even brought up the subject of sex. He helped her through that whole period after Martin when she was as low as she's ever been. And he did it all because he wanted to. She didn't even kiss him for four months – imagine that. Most guys would have done a runner inside a week. But then again, Dev is older than us and he's really clued up about things. He lets Nat be who she is rather than trying to make her into someone she's not like lots of other men do.

The reason I'm telling you all of this is that Nat's experiences are like the exact opposite of mine. I come from a really traditional Punjabi family and my dad and my three older brothers are strict as you can get. I'd never had a boyfriend before Sukh. Never even had a boy call me up at home or on my mobile. Sukh was my first foray into the world of relationships and I had Nat as my guide, wary of every move he made.

'He seems like a nice boy,' she said, about two weeks after I started seeing him. 'But if he messes you about I'll cut off his danglies with a pair of garden shears.'

'It's not him I need to worry about, Nat,' I told her.

'You on about your family?'

I nodded at her. 'Yeah. I'm going to have to be ultra-secretive. They'll kill me if I get found out.'

'Not with me around, babe. They'll have to kill me first.'

She let out a squeal – something she'd picked up from a Kung Fu movie – and then kicked out her leg, narrowly missing a cute boy in our class. The boy, Parmy, raised his eyebrows at her and then looked away when she blew him a kiss.

I looked around to make sure that no one was listening to us. Rumours had a nasty habit of getting round our school quicker than the flu.

'What if someone sees me with him?' I whispered.

Nat smiled. 'Don't shag him in public and I think you'll—'

I think the look on my face made her realize her

mistake and she started to take me more seriously. She leaned over and kissed me on the cheek. 'Sorry, Rani.'

'I hear stories all the time about girls who get spotted in town, hand in hand with their boyfriends, by interfering old hags called "auntie-ji".'

'You'll just have to be careful,' replied Nat.

'This one girl, from Coventry, got beaten up by her brothers for having a boyfriend. They locked her in her bedroom for months—'

'Let them try and do that to you,' said Nat defiantly. 'I'd be onto the coppers like a flash.'

'Believe me – with my old man, all the police would find is a dead body. Mine or his.'

'Is he really that bad?' Nat looked unconvinced.

'What about that time you came round before your first date with Dev, wearing make-up and a short dress?'

Nat grinned. 'Yeah, and did I look *sweet*, sister. Sweet like *jalebi*.'

'Well, after you went he called you a white whore and told me that I wasn't allowed to see you outside of school.'

'He spent enough time looking at my legs when I was standing in your hallway,' she replied.

'Yeah, well, he's like that, Nat. You know he is. I tell you all the time.'

'Yeah, Rani, but I never thought it was that bad. I mean, I knew it was bad but not . . . Oh, I dunno . . .'

'I don't mean to have a go but you won't ever understand, Nat. You won't ever face anything like that in your life. It's hard to comprehend if you don't live it.'

'This is beginning to sound a bit heavy, sweetie.'

'This is my life. As we know it. Three brothers who think I shouldn't speak unless I'm asking whether I should make *roti*. A father who has a coronary at the mention of anything to do with Englishness and banishes me to the kitchen whenever anything interesting is being discussed. And a mum who doesn't say a word unless it's to slag off some other family or to defend her precious favourite son, Divy.'

Nat gave me a hug. 'Oh, darling. At least you're still gorgeous and mine . . .'

'*Natalie* – is that a private hug or can we *all* have one?'

It was Mr Grimthorpe – the teacher from the pits of pervert hell. Maths lessons with him usually involved trigonometry, algebra *and* a feel of your bra as he gave you one of his special back rubs.

Nat looked at me and giggled. 'In yer dreams, wankyboy,' she muttered, just loud enough to raise a laugh but not enough for Grimthorpe to hear. Not that a lack of evidence bothered him.

'GET OUT!'

Natalie stood up, bowed to the classroom, bit her thumb theatrically at Grimthorpe, and exited the classroom like it was a stage. I sat where I was, wishing I could join her.

* * *

Sukh was waiting for me after the lesson, standing just down the corridor from the classroom. I was the first one out.

'Hey!' I said, smiling, when I saw him. I had been hoping he would be there.

'Hi – just thought I'd meet you out of class. How was it?' he asked, as I looked into his amber-coloured eyes and smiled inside.

'Oh – same old thing. Grimthorpe was being his usual self and maths is about as interesting as a family get-together at the Sikh temple.'

Sukh smiled at my joke. 'Wouldn't know,' he said. 'Don't ever go.'

'*What?*' I replied, imitating my dad. 'Calling juself the Punjabi!'

We both laughed.

Nat came striding over as we stood looking at each other.

'Hi, Nat – nice exit earlier. How are you going to pass your maths GCSE if you never stay in the class-room long enough to open your textbook?'

'Oh, stuff it. We've got another year before I've gotta worry about how many *x*s equal how many *y*s. I mean, who needs that shit, really?'

'Maths is a science . . .' I began, mimicking another maths teacher we had.

'Can't see how quadratic equations are gonna be much use to me as an actor, *dahling*.'

'That what you wanna do, yeah?' asked Sukh.

'*Absolutely*, dahling. How very sweet of you to enquire . . .' Nat grinned like a cat.

'I suppose that voice is just practice for the real thing then?' replied Sukh.

'Everything she *does* is practice,' I told him, grinning to myself.

We stood and chatted for another ten minutes and then Nat and me had to go off to English. Sukh leaned in and gave me a kiss on the cheek as we made to go and I went bright red. Nat was about to wind me up when two Punjabi girls I knew walked by.

'Eh! Check her out. Ain't you got no shame, sister?' one of them shouted.

The other one smiled slyly. 'Bet your dad don't know, innit?' she said to me.

I was about to reply but Nat butted in – just like she always does. 'Maybe, *if* you ever get rid of that acne, Jaspreet, some boy will like *you* too.'

'Piss off, you *goreeh* slag!' answered Jaspreet.

'Then again, who'd want to touch a *vicious* little cow like you?' continued Nat, totally unfazed.

The two girls turned to me. 'You best start stickin' wid your own, you know. These white girls gonna get you into shit, man.'

'Get lost.'

'Won't be saying that next time I see your mum, Rani. Checking boys an' that. Your dad's gonna kill you.'

I wanted to come back with some clever reply but what she'd just said scared me. I mean, what if she *did* tell my mum, the little bitch? I was dead.

Sukh, who'd just listened up to that point, stepped in. 'You wanna know why neither of you has got a man?' he told them. 'It's 'cos you're both so nasty. Always stirring up shit for everyone else.'

'You must like them fat, innit, Sukh,' replied Jaspreet, sneering.

'Nah – I don't think I've ever touched your mum,' said Sukh. Jaspreet's eyes hit the floor. But he didn't stop there. 'You two will live your whole lives and never be as beautiful as Rani. And the saddest thing is, you know it. That's why you chat the shit that you do. You talk about "sister" this an' "sister" that, but then you slag the other Asian girls off. No wonder nobody likes either of you.'

Nat took hold of my hand and smiled at me, motioning towards Sukh with her eyes. She knew that I was funny about my body. There were times when I felt like a whale and times when I saw what was really there. I knew I wasn't really fat, but then again . . .

The two mouthy girls walked off swearing but not replying to Sukh. As I watched them leave, upset at being called fat, I wanted to cry. I mean, I know that I had curves, but fat . . . ?

'Don't even think about it,' Sukh said to me. 'You're beautiful.'

'He's right, babe,' agreed Nat. 'I mean, those two

look like they're walking on twigs for legs. At least you've got tits and a bum. They look like little boys.'

I looked at Sukh and then at Nat but I still started to cry. Sukh looked at Nat and then at me. He put his arms around me and whispered in my ear.

'Hey, don't cry. You are the most beautiful girl I've ever seen. They're just jealous of you.'

And then just for good measure and knowing that it would cheer me up, Natalie hugged us both and started to call the two girls really nasty names in the broken Punjabi and Hindi that I had taught her over the years. '*Ben Chod, kootie, khungeriah . . .*'

I looked at Sukh and then at Nat and started laughing through my tears.

 **RANI**

'Can you make me the cup of tea, Rani?'

It was a rainy Saturday afternoon and my dad was sitting watching television. Watching but not really seeing. There was some dodgy seventies crime show on and I was bored. I headed into the kitchen and put a pan of water on to boil. The tea my dad wanted was traditional Punjabi tea, made by boiling water and then adding tea bags and letting it simmer and stew for about half an hour with a handful of cloves and some cinnamon bark. Once the liquid had simmered I added about a cupful of milk and loads of sugar and brought it back to the boil. Outside, the rain was coming down in sheets and pounding against the kitchen window so hard I thought the window would break. The sky was the colour of slate and there were huge ominous-looking clouds gathering, all varying shades of grey.

I poured out the tea and went back into the living room. My brothers were attending to the family business, a hosiery factory and a couple of retail out-lets in town. My dad had all but retired and had let my brothers take over the business he had built from scratch since coming to Leicester from the Punjab, back in the sixties. He had come over nearly ten years before my mum, which was why they had had children so late. I was the last in the line, born seven years after Gurdip, the youngest of my brothers. Being so much younger than my brothers *and* being a girl pretty much guaranteed that I got left out of family stuff, unless it was going to boring weddings. They never talked business around me, assuming, correctly, that I couldn't care less. Most of my friends' parents were much younger than mine and sometimes I wished that my parents were younger too. Maybe they'd be less traditional. But then again, there was probably nothing that would make my parents the liberal dream that I wanted them to be. It just wasn't in their nature.

I was waiting for my mum to come back. She had nipped to a neighbour's to pick up some material for a wedding outfit she was making. I had a plan that involved telling her that I had to go and get something from town and I needed her to say I could. I know it sounds sad but I had to have permission and a good reason to go into town. My parents weren't happy about me going on my own, not even with Natalie. *Especially* not with Natalie. I had it all worked out. My success at school depended on a trip to the stationer's in town and my mobile phone company were ripping me off so I needed to talk to them too. I kind of forgot to mention that Sukh had sent me a text message telling me that he was in town and asking could I meet up with him?

My dad yawned as I passed him his tea and then he looked me up and down before speaking in Punjabi. 'Haven't you got any work to do?' he said.

'No, ji,' I told him, being respectful as always.

'No homework from school? No housework? It's not good for a girl to just sit around doing nothing. It doesn't look good, Rani.'

I sighed and said that I'd try to find something to do. I was just walking out of the living room when my mum came in through the front door.

'Mum, I need to go into town,' I said in English.

My mum, dressed in a traditional Punjabi suit, looked worn out. The flecks of grey in her pulled-back hair were growing more prominent each week. Her face looked drawn too.

'Are you feeling OK?' I asked as she walked into the kitchen.

'You're not a *goreeh* yet,' she told me in Punjabi. 'Speak the language you were born to speak.'

I forgot about enquiring after her welfare and told her about the phone company and the stationery I needed.

'Every week you have something else to do in town. Go on, go if you have to, but if I hear that you're mess-ing about like those other girls . . .'

'I'm not, Mum – I promise.'

The 'other girls' my mum was talking about didn't

exist as individuals that she actually knew. The phrase was a collective shorthand for all the ills of western society – bad girls who tried to be English and went out with boys and got pregnant. Smoked like men and drank like them too. The kind of girls who were the subjects of gossip between the older women at the *gurudwara* and all the family gatherings that occurred – weddings, parties and even funerals. The girls who ran off with Muslim boys or left home and ended up in council flats, leaving their family *izzat* in the gutter. There were countless stories about such girls and my mum was always warning me about the consequences of 'messing about', as she put it. To call my home life restrictive was not even half way to the truth. I felt like I was living in a open prison: I was allowed out but always had to return at the end of the day. It's a bit like caging a hungry animal and placing a bowl of food just out of reach. Not that I was hungry or an animal, but you know what I mean. Once the animal gets out it wants all the food it can get – just to make up for being deprived previously.

I went up to my bedroom and sent Sukh a text back, arranging to meet him in town. Somewhere away from the main shopping centres where my brothers would be working in the shops we owned. I really didn't want them to see me with Sukh, especially not Divy, my eldest brother, who I didn't get on with too well. I chose an area called The Lanes – a mish-mash of narrow streets and alleyways that housed trendy little boutiques and coffee shops and bars. There was a café bar that had opened earlier in the year, and Natalie's sister Jasmine worked there. I wanted to be able to just sit down and talk to Sukh without worrying about who might see us. The bar had a nice dimly lit section at the back where you could watch the world go by without anyone noticing you. Natalie and me spent countless afternoons in there hassling Jasmine for free coffees and, if we were feeling naughty, a sneaky tequila or vodka. Not that we drank much. Just every now and then.

I got to the bar before Sukh and ordered a coffee. Jasmine was due back from a break so I went and sat near the door, so that Sukh would see me when he came in. I didn't have to wait long. He was right on time, which is an attribute that I like. He smiled when he saw me and I stood up as he approached, ready to give him a hug and a kiss. On the lips. I felt a bit self-conscious as I did it, even though the place was empty apart from another couple and an Asian guy who was reading the *Guardian* and drinking a beer. But Sukh kissed me back and then touched my cheek lightly, smiling and looking into my eyes. I shivered and then my heart skipped another beat. There was something about the way he looked at me that made me feel warm inside. Soppy, I know. But true.

I noticed his hair. 'What have you done to your hair?'

'Had it cut – why, don't you like it?' he replied, running his hand through what was left of it.

It was shaved short to his head and on most guys it would have looked thuggish but with his big brown eyes and friendly smile it just looked really neat and sharp, despite the rain.

'No, no. It's lovely,' I assured him.

'Only I can go back and get the girl who cut it to stick the bits back on if you like.'

I smiled and called him an arse and then I asked him what he wanted to drink. He looked around and then straight at me. I shivered again and then told myself to get it together. I mean, *really*.

'I'll get it,' he said.

'No – don't be macho about it. What do you want?'

'A coffee then. Black.'

'I'll just order it.'

I walked over to the bar and saw Jasmine behind it, emptying bags of change into one of the tills. Jasmine was shorter than Nat but even more beautiful if that was possible. She had shoulder-length brown hair that she was growing out and olive skin with sparkling green and hazel eyes the same colour as mine. She always looked wonderful too, immaculately turned out and always well dressed. She saw me and smiled.

'Hey, babe – how are you?' she asked, coming over.

'I'm fine. In here with my man,' I replied, a feeling of warmth coming over me as I said the words 'my man'. I'd never been able to say that before.

'The one Nat keeps going on about?'

'Yeah – he's over there.' I nodded in Sukh's direction.

Jasmine looked over to Sukh and then back at me. 'Very nice. Has he got a brother?'

I laughed and ordered Sukh's drink. Jasmine told me to go and sit down.

'I'll bring it over when it's ready.'

When she eventually walked over Sukh smiled at her and said hello. I watched her walk away in her blue jeans and red T-shirt with an Elvis Presley motif and wished that I could wear my clothes as well as she did. Sukh watched her too.

'Do you think she's pretty?' I asked him, waiting to see how he would react. Was he going to lie and say no because he thought I'd get upset or was he going to be honest?

He smiled and raised a single eyebrow at me. 'She's beautiful, but I'm not here to talk about her. I'm here to be with you.'

Passed with honours.

We spent about two hours talking about everything and anything. I told him about my parents and how I'd had to lie to them about coming into town. I told him about my three brothers, Divy, Raj and Gurdip, who were all really traditional when it came to me.

'They gonna beat me up if they see us together,' he said, smiling to himself.

'That's exactly what they would do too – so don't be messing me about, boy.'

'Like I would,' he said, before telling me about his own family and his sister Parvy, who owned a flat in Leicester but was working in New York – talk about cool.

'She gave me the keys to her flat before she went. I go over and water the plants and that,' he told me.

'She gave *you* the keys?' I said, imagining wild parties.

'Yeah – why not?' replied Sukh, looking a little hurt. 'I'm very responsible. Ain't like I take my mates round. I just chill out there when I need to get away from the house.'

'That's really nice of her,' I said quickly. I hadn't meant to imply that he was untrustworthy. It was just a bit different, that's all. Different and very promising, I thought to myself.

'You wanna go see it?' asked Sukh, smiling.

'Erm, yes, I'd love to,' I replied.

'Cool. It's only down King Street. Drink up and we'll walk over. I need to water her plants anyway.'

I looked at my watch and panicked. 'What? Now?' I stuttered, instantly embarrassed at my reaction.

'Yeah – why not? Don't worry, Rani – I don't mean to . . . you know – not *that*. Just want you to see it.'

'I didn't think that, Sukh,' I told him. 'I just can't. Not today. I told my mum I'd only be a couple of hours. I'll have to go and see Raj in the shop – get him to give me a lift home.'

Sukh looked like he was going to try and persuade me to go with him. Or so I thought. But in the end he smiled and walked some of the way with me.

'You don't mind?' I asked him, worried that he might be disappointed.

'Not at all. There'll be other times.'

'Call me later then?'

He smiled and planted a big kiss on my lips. 'It's weird but I can't not call you. It's like I can't stop thinking about you when I'm not with you.'

Now, some girls I know would have run a mile if he had said that to them – called him clingy or something similar. But the idea that he thought about me as much as I thought about him made me feel good inside. I smiled like the Cheshire Cat and kissed him back.

'You're doing well, young man,' I told him jokingly. 'Keep it up and you never know . . .'

I floated off towards my dad's shop without a care in the world.

 **RANI**

'Where you goin' now?' asked my brother Gurdip as I checked my hair in the hall mirror.

'What's it got to do with you?' I said, picking up my bag and heading into the lounge, where Divy was watching telly and drinking beer.

I looked at him and felt like shaking my head. Gangster wannabe. Gurdip, who had followed me, had three days' worth of stubble on his face and his belly was hanging over his shiny tracksuit bottoms, which he wore with a sweatshirt that was two sizes too small. And to cap it off the shirt said LOOK BUT DON'T TOUCH. Yeah – as if.

'Everything, innit,' Gurdip told me. 'I'm responsible for you while Mum and Dad are in Birmingham.' He eyed my bag with suspicion.

'Ain't you got nothing better to do?' I asked him.

My two eldest brothers were married but Gurdip was still single and lived at home with us. Not that Divy and Raj lived far away – they'd both bought houses on the same street.

My parents were away and I was on my way to see

Sukh. We'd been together for nearly six months now and saw each other regularly at school and as often as I could manage it outside. It was hard because my brothers watched me like hawks, on the orders of my dad. To me it was just another example of my macho brothers' idea of responsibility and of my father's hypocrisy: my stupid brothers could do what they wanted, even when they were younger, but I had to be home by set times and couldn't go to parties and stuff. Being a Punjabi girl with parents like mine isn't easy, believe me.

'Watch your mouth, Rani. You need to get some respect—' warned Gurdip, stifling a belch.

'Yeah – for me,' I replied instantly.

But Gurdip either didn't hear what I said or chose to ignore it. Instead he tapped his watch and looked across at Divy. 'You best be back by five – wherever you goin'. Don't make me have to call you or they'll be trouble, innit.'

'I think you mean "there will", not "they will",' I replied.

'Don't push it, Rani. You ain't no *goreeh*,' said Divy, getting involved just to wind me up.

'Yeah, yeah,' I said, dismissing him with a wave of my hand.

'An' you best not be getting up to no good with that dutty white gal,' added Divy.

'She ain't dirty and last I checked you weren't a Jamaican, so what's with the accent?' I glared at him.

'Seen her with some Indian guy, innit, kissing like she ain't got no shame, man. Anyhow, I hear about *you* doin' that shit – you're *dead*.'

Sukh's face flashed through my mind and my stomach knotted a little. I walked out of the house, calling my brothers all the names I could think of, muttering under my breath like some mad woman. The bus took ages to get into town from Oadby. The main road was clogged with traffic because there was a race meeting and, further into town, a demonstration against the city council.

At the train station I spotted an uncle of mine standing by his cab talking to other men in turbans. Seeing a member of my family made me think about what Divy had said and what would happen if I got caught with Sukh. I had such a large family that the chances of being seen by some aunt or cousin were quite high. But in a way the threat of being caught out made it all seem so much more intense. Even though Sukh was from the same background as me and everything, I would still get murdered by my dad if someone caught us together. It didn't matter that he was a Punjabi, he was still a *boy*! And the only time I was supposed to even begin to think about boys or men was on the day that I acted like a good Punjabi girl and married some fat, hairy bloater, chosen for me by a panel of haggard matchmakers who always smelled of onions and garlic and turned up at every Punjabi social occasion. I doubt my dad could even imagine us kissing or anything else. It was the stuff of his nightmares.

I met Sukh in the café bar where Jasmine worked and, with my brother's threat echoing in my head, I gave him a long, hard kiss as soon as I saw him – kind of like sticking two fingers up at my family. Sukh was taken aback and for a moment I felt as if I had messed up somehow. But it was just a fleeting thing and he quickly kissed me back. When he let me go I had to get my head to reattach itself to my shoulders.

'You look beautiful,' he told me as we sat down, still holding hands.

'I think you need your eyes testing,' I said, going a shade of pink.

'Not me, honey. I hope when you look in the mirror you see "fit bird",' he continued, smiling.

'Bird? And there was I thinking you were a nice boy . . .' I was joking of course. And flattered.

We ordered coffee, then sat and chatted for ages. It was as though we had always known each other. He knew exactly how to talk to me and listened with real interest to everything I said. And he told me everything, from what he'd done all day to how he felt about things. Yes, that's right. A boy. Talking about feelings. He'd been like that from day one – sensitive, attentive, caring. It was boyfriend heaven, according to Nat.

And as he spoke his eyes sparkled and his hands were all over the place, helping to explain what he meant. I was almost in a trance, spellbound by his every word, watching his hands spell out stories. I was feeling something I had never known before – something that hadn't existed in my life. A warm, surging force of emotion towards another person. I was in love.

Not the kind of love that you have for your family or your best friend. Not like that. This was pure, heart-stopping, can't-think-about-anyone-else stuff. But as soon as I had decided on what I was feeling, I began to feel stupid and silly and just a little insecure. I started thinking about negatives. What if he didn't like me as much as I liked him? What if he was putting on a front and turned out to be a wanker like Martin? As nice as it was to be alone with Sukh without Natalie popping up out of nowhere, I could have done with her being there, guiding me through a minefield to which I didn't have a map. But then who does?

'D'you wanna go chill out at the flat?' said Sukh, looking at his watch. 'Parvy's in New York.'

I looked at him blankly for a moment.

'Are you OK, Rani?' he said getting out of his seat.

'Yeah – just thinking—'

'About how gorgeous I am?' he said, laughing.

'Actually – I was,' I replied, smiling. 'Yeah, let's go to your sister's flat – but no funny business, young man.'

'*Funny? Me?* You must have someone else in mind, Rani. I'm really nice, me,' he told me, grinning.

He held out his hand and helped me up, kissing me on the cheek. We walked out of the café and through

49

The Lanes to Market Street. As we walked I held Sukh's hand tightly, as though he'd float away if I didn't cling onto him.

The entrance to Parvy's building was down a narrow lane off King Street. It was an old hosiery mill, converted into expensive flats for young professionals with money – the kind of independent, successful young women that I sometimes dreamed of becoming. Other times I saw myself with a family, in a nice house, after a wonderful, colourful marriage to the man of my dreams, with red and gold silks and laughing relatives and, eventually, beautiful, happy children. It was nice to dream – it was a way of putting out of my mind the reality of my life. My father would be more than happy to pack me off to the first rich Asian family that came knocking. People who 'fitted' our family; came from exactly the same background and had the same wealth.

As we took a small lift up to the top of the building, I wondered what my dad would make of someone like Sukh and his family. He'd probably laugh to himself and tell me that Sukh's dad had sold his family's *izzat* down the river in the quest to become 'bloody *goreh*'. That his sister was a *khungeri* – a whore who didn't respect Punjabi traditions and thought she was different from other Punjabi women.

'*Apna aap nu sammage thei ki heh?*' he'd say. 'Who does she think she is?'

The door to Parvy's flat was wide and made of solid, heavy-looking wood. There was a buzzer and a spy hole but Sukh pulled out his own key and opened the door. The flat was immaculate, like something from a TV makeover show but with more style. I suppose you could have called it minimalist – all neutral walls and clutter free – a million miles from my parents' house, where every space was filled with porcelain figurines and the walls were covered in gold-framed photos of family and gurus. The floors were solid light wood all the way through and even though it was actually quite small, a huge skylight in the middle of the living-room ceiling made it feel light and airy. I was so jealous. It was my fifth or sixth visit and my reaction was the same each time. I wanted one just like it.

Sukh made himself comfortable on the sofa in front of a huge television and turned it on. 'What do you wanna watch?' he asked, as I sat down next to him, admiring the stone head that sat on its own in a corner.

'I don't mind,' I said. 'We don't have to watch a DVD. We could just talk.'

Sukh pulled a face and got up, walking over to a stand of CDs and movies, picking out a plastic case. 'Yeah, we could talk, but I'm a bloke,' he said, mocking me. 'I don't wanna talk.'

'What's that you've got?' I enquired.

'It's a film called *True Romance* – wicked!'

'Isn't that a chick flick, Sukh?' I asked.

'You could call it that,' he replied. 'A chick flick with Mafia, murder and mayhem . . .' He'd lowered his voice, stressing the 'm's on each of the three words, as if he were doing a film-trailer voice-over.

'You're so funny,' I said, smiling. 'Maybe you should take up acting with Natalie.'

'Nah — I wanna go to Bollywood, not Hollywood. Be the big star of the *moovee*, innit.' This time he sounded like one of my brothers. I got up and walked to him, pinching him on the arm.

'*Oww!*'

'Oh quit it — you big girl. Just put the DVD in and come and sit down,' I told him, returning to the sofa.

'Oh jess, boss — anyting ju seh pleese.'

'And keep that bhangra-boy accent for your mates.'

Sukh put the DVD in and turned round before jumping on me.

'GERROFF!' I screamed as he tickled my sides, right where he knew would make the most impact. By the time he'd stopped I was breathless and red, and my hair was all over the place, not to mention my clothes.

'Oh — look what you've done,' I said. 'I look like a bag lady now.'

'*Beautiful* bag lady—'

'You do need to get those eyes tested,' I told him, laughing.

He didn't laugh back. Instead he pulled me to him and I could feel the heat of his breath on my face. I held back for a split second and then we were kissing.

I don't know how we ended up with no clothes on but it just seemed to happen. Neither of us had planned it – it just felt right to be doing what we were doing. Part of me wanted to stop. Another bit of me wanted to carry on, like the caged animal, suddenly freed, with a mountain of food before it. I kissed his mouth, then his neck and his chest as he caressed my breasts really gently and then kissed them. I thought I was going to explode inside when I felt his tongue touch me . . . it was like a dream.

Later, fully dressed, we lay on the sofa together, watching the film. I was listening to his heartbeat and my head was light from what we had just done. I didn't want to move. I just wanted to lie where I was for as long as possible and listen to the thump, thump, thump of my beautiful boyfriend's heart and feel his warmth next to me. I wanted to kiss him some more and tell him that I'd really meant it earlier, when I had told him that I loved him. As the film wore on, I really didn't pay it that much attention, although it looked fantastic. I just lay there lost in my own sweet thoughts, my mind's eye full of blue, cloudless skies and my senses full of the sweet smell of summer flowers.

Eventually I kissed the tip of one of his ears and whispered to him. 'You know what I said . . .' I began, as he turned to look me in the eye.

'I know,' he said. 'I love you, Rani Sandhu. I love you too.'

I think he was slightly embarrassed because some-thing crossed his eyes and then he buried his face in my neck before I pulled it back towards my own.

'You're not just saying that – because of what we did?' I asked him.

'I can't go for five minutes without thinking about you, Rani,' he replied. 'I've never felt the feelings that I have for you. It's like we've been together for ever – God, if my mates could hear me now . . .' He laughed a little, maybe to cover up his confusion.

'It feels like we were meant to be together, Rani,' he continued. 'So, no, I'm not just saying it because of earlier – I promise.'

That was enough for me. I kissed him some more and then settled back down to watch the film, only for my eye to catch the flashing display on the front of the DVD player.

17.46 . . . 17.46 . . . 17.46.

'SHIT!'

I jumped up, knocking Sukh to the floor, panicked. I was supposed to have been home for five. My brother was going to go mental.

'What?' said Sukh as I grabbed my bag and ran to the bathroom.

'I told Gurdip I'd be back for five,' I told him. 'He's going to do his nut.'

'Don't worry about it . . .' began Sukh before realizing that he was on dangerous ground. His family were OK – mine were not. Instead of continuing he got up off the floor and began to tidy up, ready for us to leave. 'Come on, I'll walk you to the cab stand over the road,' he said.

'I haven't got enough money for a cab,' I said, walking back into the living-room area with my hair back to its tidy best. 'I need to go to a cash point.'

Sukh took my hand. 'I've got some, honey.'

We made our way out into the street and walked across to the cab stand, hand in hand. There was a cab waiting and I told him where I wanted to go before turning to Sukh.

'Call me later?' I asked, kissing him on the mouth.

'Just try and stop me,' he said, giving me a big hug.

'What you up to tomorrow?'

'Football — Sunday League game against the enemy.'

'Who?'

Sukh laughed. 'Never mind, Rani. It's boy stuff — bhangra, Bacardi and football.'

I turned up my nose, kissed him again and got into the taxi. As the car pulled away I watched Sukh, standing there watching me.

The driver, a balding middle-aged white man, let out a chuckle. 'Yer boyfriend, is he?' he asked in a thick Leicester accent.

'Yes,' I said, smiling broadly. 'Yes, he is.'

'Doon't offen see Asian kids kissin' in daylight — d'yer famleh know about 'im?'

I looked at the driver, wondering if he was trying to

take the mickey, but in the end I just answered his question. 'No, no they don't. And do you know what? I couldn't care less – I'm in love.'

The driver chuckled some more out of the side of his mouth, as he swerved to avoid another car. 'How lovely is that. Valentine's on the way an' all . . .'

I was floating on a cloud all the way home, smiling to myself as I thought about what Natalie was going to say.

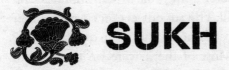 **SUKH**

Sukh sat on the side of the football pitch, cleaning his boots as he waited for his chance to get into the action. The pitch sat on a slope in the middle of Victoria Park. There were about a hundred people gathered around it, most of them Punjabi and all male. The two teams were Asian, with one affiliated to a Sikh temple on East Park Road, and the other to a rival *guruduara* just on the outskirts of the city centre. Sukh was playing for the city centre team, or at least he would have been if he'd been picked. Instead he was one of the substitutes, waiting to get on. The team was managed by one of his cousins and was full of his relatives. Sukh had never played for the first team before and was quite excited. Most of the players came from families called Bains or Johal. On the opposite team, run by a bearded alcoholic called Jit, the players were mainly Rais, with a few Sandhus and one or two Gills thrown in. Not that the surnames meant much. They were amongst the five most popular names in the British Punjabi community, all linked to different villages back in the Punjab.

The game had been going for twenty minutes and the score was one all. The supporters faced each other across the pitch, occasionally shouting an insult one way or the other. Most of them were on the way to getting pissed, with bottles of Bacardi and Coke cans being passed around. There were one or two there who didn't drink, mainly older men, but all the youngsters were at it. It was part of the fun. The game was like a Punjabi version of Celtic–Rangers or Liverpool–Everton. There was an intense rivalry between the teams, based, as far as Sukh could make out, on a similar rivalry between the two *gurudwaras*. That was what Sukh didn't get. Most of the lads playing the game or watching never went to the temple, unless it was to a wedding, and even that would just be a precursor to the piss-up afterwards. Yet four times a year they got together and 'stood up' for their temple of choice. Defending their side and their reputation often led to fighting, nasty tackles and the throwing of missiles onto the pitch. Already the game had produced four yellow cards and one of the opposite team had been carried off with an ankle injury. There was a unspoken feud between the two sides, one which Sukh had avoided so far.

'Ain't gonna need to put them boots on, man – you ain't no good,' came a familiar voice from behind Sukh.

He turned his head to see a cousin of his, Tej, carrying a bottle of Pils and smiling inanely.

'All right, Coz,' smiled Sukh, wondering how pissed Tej was. He was well known for being half lit most of the time. In the language of Punjabi football culture, he was a 'good lad'.

'*All right? Salehyah* – we don't say "all right" – we say "*Aww kiddah!*"'

He shouted the last bit and then did a little bhangra jig, going round in a wide arcing circle, bumping into some of the other supporters, all either family or friends, spilling his beer.

Sukh shook his head and laughed as another cousin, Manj, grabbed Tej in a head lock and wrestled him to the ground, knocking his beer out of his hands. Both of them ended up rolling in the grass, getting their clothes dirty, like children half their age. After a few minutes of this both cousins got up and dusted themselves off, grinning. Tej looked for his beer, which had spilled out on the grass. He picked up the empty bottle, inspected it, shrugged and threw it away. Then he opened up his jacket, took a fresh bottle from an inside pocket and opened it with his teeth, making Sukh wince. He drank half of it down in one go. Manj took it from him and finished it before belching at Sukh.

'You two are crazy,' laughed Sukh, getting up from the ground.

'Nah – we's just havin' a laff, that's all,' smiled Manj, the taller of the two cousins, with powerful shoulders, big arms and even bigger belly. His un-ironed jeans were stained and his Nike trainers sat like boats at the end of his surprisingly skinny legs. He wiped his black leather jacket and then cuffed Sukh around the head, catching his ear and making it sting.

'*Ow!*'

'Ah shut up, you pussy,' laughed Manj. 'You a man or what, man?'

'Fat bastard,' mumbled Sukh before turning his attention back to the game.

On the pitch two players were trading insults in Punjabi as their team mates held them back. Sukh wondered what had caused the argument. He turned to yet another cousin, Ranjit, and asked him what was going on.

'Them wankers just chopped him down, innit. Man's too fast for that fat twat they got playin' right back — so he just chopped him.'

Sukh watched as the right back for the opposing team, a short, stocky bloke with a bald head, aimed a head butt at their player, a skinny winger called Jag, who was fast like a greyhound. The ref and some of the other players dragged the right back away and then he was red carded. He threw a punch at the ref as soon as he saw the card, catching him right in the middle of his jaw and knocking him out cold. And then all hell broke loose. Both teams and both sets of supporters ran onto the pitch and began to fight. There were bottles being thrown and punches flying through the air. Sukh, shocked by how quickly things had deteriorated, just sat and watched. He heard a police siren, and then another, from the direction of London Road, patrol cars that must have been passing by and seen the fighting.

And then, just as quickly as it had begun, the fighting stopped and the two sides returned to their own touchlines. The policemen, running up to the pitch, went immediately to the referee, who had been revived. He spoke to the officers and then to the two managers, before abandoning the game. The police arrested the stocky right back and returned to their cars with their prisoner and a sore ref in tow.

A huge groan went up when the coach for Sukh's side came over and told them. Accusations were thrown towards the opposing team, threats of violence. Eventually the players went to their cars, parked on London Road opposite a pub called the Old Horse, and got changed, standing in the lee of passenger doors, as some of the spectators went home. The rest crossed the busy road and headed for the pub — supporters from both sides walking side by side but ignoring each other.

Sukh stood by Ranjit's Vectra as bhangra music pounded the speakers. He pulled out his mobile, wondering what Rani was doing, and started to send her a text message, but cancelled it quickly when Ranjit took an interest.

'Who you sendin' messages, little cousin? You got yourself some skirt?' he said, looking at Sukh's phone.

'Just checkin' to see if anyone called me,' Sukh

replied, as Manj and Tej came over and gestured towards the pub.

'Might as well go down the pub, innit – them fuckers ruined the football,' said Tej, spitting after his sentence.

'Might as well, at that,' agreed Ranjit.

'Ain't it gonna kick off in there with them and us around?' Sukh asked, worried that the fight would move to the pub.

'Nah – it's just a football thing, innit,' Ranjit told him.

'An' even if it does,' added Manj, smiling, 'ain't stopping me from goin' in. I'll fight 'em if it comes down to it.'

'Them an' their sisters,' laughed Tej.

Ranjit smiled, showing a gold tooth, and played with his gold chain. 'Fight their sisters?' he said. 'What I'd do to 'em – dunno if you could *call* that fightin', innit.'

'The girls or the lads?' asked Tej.

'I'm ready to batter their men *and* tek them women,' said Manj.

'Why all the fightin' and shit – it's just a footie game, innit?' asked Sukh.

'Don't worry yourself, Sukhy,' Ranjit told him. 'There's history here, man – them bastards got it coming.'

'What history?'

'Never mind – you is too young, innit. Just lef' it – ain't nuttin' happening anyway. Most of them mans is just talk, you get me?'

Sukh shook his head at Ranjit's mix of accents and wondered what the hell he was talking about. He knew there was rivalry between the two sets of supporters but had no idea what it was about. As far as Sukh knew it had always been there. In the end he decided to leave it and stood outside the pub whilst Manj and Tej went in to get some drinks. They came back out with eight bottles of Pils.

'Nah,' said Sukh, shaking his head, 'I asked for a Coke, man.'

Ranjit snorted. 'Drink the beer, Coz,' he said. 'You with us, innit. We's all family here. Don't worry, we'll make sure you get home all right.'

'But—' began Sukh, only to have Tej cut him off.

'Leave it, kid,' he said, smiling. 'Mek we drink these and then we'll take you home.'

Sukh felt for his mobile in the back pocket of his jeans, wishing he had just gone home or called Rani. But then, as two bottles of beer were thrust in his hands, he decided to have a drink. After all, he was with his family and he'd told Rani he would call her later. He took a swig and joined in with his cousins, listening as they told dirty stories. They continued that way for about forty minutes, with others coming over to join them, before Ranjit told Sukh that he'd drop him off at home.

'Wait, man,' shouted Manj, as Sukh and Ranjit walked across the road to Ranjit's car.

'Give us a lift too,' added Tej, finishing his fourth beer.

'Come on then, you nutters,' agreed Ranjit. 'Let's go.'

 **RANI**

'Do you think I'm a slag?' I asked Natalie, as she sat on the other end of the phone line, speechless for the first time ever.

'Er . . .'

'Oh *please* don't say "er", Nat. How come the one time I *need* you to say something, you can't speak? Can't shut you up normally.'

'It's just a bit of a shock, that's all, babe,' she replied.

I smiled to myself. The real Nat was on her way back after the initial surprise.

'You know,' she continued, 'one minute you're just holding hands and the next . . .'

'It was just as much a shock for me,' I told her. Well, it was *true*.

'So how did it happen?'

'We were sitting on the sofa, messing about, like you do . . .'

'Like *you* do, obviously—'

'Natalie, will you listen?'

'Sorry, babe – couldn't resist. Carry on.'

'That's just it. We were messing about and we started

65

kissing and the next thing—'

'You were on the floor with no clothes on?'

'Natalie!'

'But that's how it happened, right?'

'Well . . . yes. But I never *meant* for it to . . .'

'I'm not saying that you did. *Mean* it, I mean.'

'See? You do think I'm a slag. You've even forgotten how to string a sentence together.'

'Well – what did you think I would do? I mean, it's *great*, if it's what you want. I'm all happy for you, honest. It's just that . . . Well, it's just not *like* you. I'm the naughty one. You're sweet, angelic Rani – my innocent sidekick. I'm not sure how this is going to affect the dynamic of our relationship, darling . . .'

'Nat – what the *hell* are you talking about?'

'Well . . . You. Being—'

'What? A slag?'

'No – just not the same . . .'

'But I haven't *changed*,' I pleaded.

'I'm not saying that you have but—'

'Hang on, Nat – someone's at my door . . .'

I put the handset down and jumped off my bed to see who was there. It was my mum.

'Here, have some fruit,' she said in Punjabi.

'I don't want any,' I replied, eyeing the brown banana and wrinkled apple.

'*Beteh*, it's from the *gurudwara* – *prashad* – you must have some . . .'

I took the apple and closed the door. *Prashad* is the

name for anything blessed during a Sikh prayer – often it's old fruit that some old dear has brought along. I mean, how am I supposed to know what's in it? Could be anything. I picked up my school bag and shoved the apple in and then picked up the handset, plonking myself down on my bed again.

'Hey, babe,' I said. 'Sorry about that.'

'Who was it – Mummy-ji?'

'Yeah – same old nonsense . . .'

'Never mind. Anyway as I was saying—'

'You were calling me a slag.'

'Rani – I wasn't calling you anything. I wouldn't – I love you . . .'

'But you said I wouldn't be the same.'

'Yeah, but only in the sense that when I talk about Dev's "William" now, instead of going red and telling me to quit it – you'll be telling me all about Sukh's . . .'

'I will not.'

'Maybe not – but do you see what I mean?'

'You know, you haven't even asked me once how I feel about it . . .'

'I'm sorry. How do you feel?'

'It's not the same now. You've *got* to ask because I told you that you hadn't asked. You're only asking because you feel guilty—'

'Rani, you're beginning to sound like a child now . . .'

'Oh, go and boil your head, you witch!'

There was a silence for maybe ten seconds and then we both started laughing.

'If I was a witch,' said Nat, 'I'd be a damn sexy one.'

'I'm sorry, honey,' I replied. 'I didn't mean it . . .'

'Look, this is stupid. Come round to mine.'

'I dunno if my mum will let me,' I said.

'You haven't even asked her. Can't you say that I'm a new girl – call me Pritpaljit Kaur or something . . .?'

'Let me ask her and I'll call you back.'

'You'd better, you little witch, you.'

'I'm not a—'

But the line had already gone dead. I sat and thought about an excuse for going to see Natalie. An excuse that my mum would go for. In the end I picked up my school bag, stuffed in a couple of maths text-books and went downstairs, holding the wrinkled apple from earlier in my hand.

'Mum, I'm going to Parvinder's house to do my homework.' Just for extra points I took a bite of the apple. Just a small one.

'Parvinder? I've never heard her name before,' replied my mum, but not with any real suspicion. She was too busy watching some Bollywood film on the telly.

I pulled out my textbooks. 'Maths,' I said, showing her the books.

'Go on then, but be back by six and don't turn off your mobile phone,' she said.

My dad, who had been sitting opposite my mum the whole time, yawned, farted and showed no interest.

'But finish your *prashad* first,' added my mum.

'I'll eat it on the way,' I shouted as I was already at the front door. I put my bag over my shoulder and ran down the long driveway and out into the street. Waiting until I got to the first junction with another road, I chucked the apple into a bush and spat out the piece I had bitten off. I pulled out my phone and rang Natalie.

'Hey!' she answered on the first ring.

'On my way round, baby,' I said, giggling like a little girl and instantly annoying myself. But I was in such a good mood. I was young, happy and in love. Enough to annoy anyone, I reckon. Not that I cared.

'Jasmine's here and my mum's cooked dinner – there might even be a bit left.'

'Get me a plate ready then,' I said, flipping my phone shut and grinning to myself.

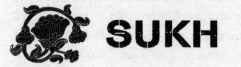 **SUKH**

As Ranjit's car rounded Beckingham Road onto Evington Road Sukh took out his mobile again, hoping that Rani had called or sent a message but there was nothing. He put it back again and listened to the beat of the bhangra tune pumping out of the stereo. The tune was big, getting played on Radio One no less, although listening to the DJs as they tried to pronounce the title made Sukh laugh. They didn't have a clue how to say it properly, but then most of them probably never thought they'd be playing Punjabi folk music on prime-time radio. It was an OK tune, too. Not really Sukh's thing but then he wasn't really that into bhangra – it was something he didn't mind, but given the choice he was a garage boy. And hip-hop.

Rani hated bhangra with a passion, which had surprised Sukh. Most of the Punjabi girls at school were into it big time – they had all the latest CDs and that – but then Rani didn't really hang about with the other Punjabi girls. She was into the same stuff as her friend Natalie, which wasn't that surprising. Coldplay

70

and stuff like that. CDs that Nat nicked from her older sister, Jasmine. Sukh smiled to himself as he remembered Rani talking about dancing the bhangra.

'It's all sowing the seed and changing light bulbs and stuff, isn't it?' she'd said.

Sukh had mocked her about being a 'white' girl, but only for a laugh. It didn't really matter to him what she didn't like as long as she continued to like him. Lost in his thoughts he didn't notice that the car had pulled over by the mosque at the bottom of Evington Road until his cousins had started to open doors and get out.

'Best get ready – there's a few of them now,' growled Tej, as he got out. Sukh suddenly forgot all about Rani. He was wondering what was up.

Manj told him to stay in the car.

'But—' began Sukh.

'I said stay in the car, Sukh,' Manj cut in sternly.

Sukh did as he was told but leaned forward to turn the music down so that he could hear what was being said. Ranjit had parked the car about twenty-five metres ahead of a group of other Punjabi youths who were walking towards it.

Tej growled at Manj again. 'You got my back this time?' he asked.

'You ain't gotta worry about me,' replied Manj, grinning, but not in a nice way.

'Let's wind them up,' said Ranjit, as they approached. He waited until they were within earshot before speaking, without looking at them directly.

'Mother used to be a whore,' he said, leaning non-chalantly on the bonnet.

'Yeah – sister too,' added Tej.

One of the other youths, a big, stocky lad, stopped and looked at Tej. He obviously knew him. 'You talkin' 'bout my mum, Tej?' he demanded, his eyes blazing.

'We're talking about *someone's* mum,' replied Manj.

'I said, are you talking about *my* mum?' repeated the youth.

Manj and Tej looked at the youth, each other and then at Ranjit, who smiled.

'We're not talking about *your* mum – just *someone's* mum. Why – you wanna make something of it, Pete?' said Ranjit.

The youth, Pete, looked at his mates and then back at Ranjit, his fists clenching by his side. 'Do *you* wanna make something of it?' he countered.

'I ain't starting *nothing*, but that don't mean I won't batter you if something starts,' replied Ranjit, with a smug look.

'Only thing you're battering is a fish—'

Another car screeched up, this one full of men from the same clan as Pete and his gang.

'*Ah ki hoondah?*' said one of the men in Punjabi, wanting to know what was going on.

'These Bains got something to say, Divy,' said one of the youths with Pete.

The man got out of the car, a shiny black Audi A6, and walked up to Tej, Ranjit and Manj. From the look on their faces, Sukh could tell that they were scared of him.

'That right, Tej?' asked the man, ponytailed and dressed in black leather, his neck and wrists dripping with gold chains, huge gold sovereigns on his meaty fingers.

'It's nothing, rude bwoi,' replied Tej. 'No need for any trouble—'

'*What?* You talk shit to them but now we're here you wanna let it go? Ain't you got the heart for it . . . ?'

Manj put his hand inside his pocket, quietly and quickly, and before anyone could blink he pulled out a flick knife. 'BACK OFF!' he shouted, moving between Tej and the ponytailed man.

For a moment everything was still and then the man spat to the floor and told the youths with Pete to go home. He turned to Manj, who still had hold of the knife but obviously wasn't going to use it.

'You fucking Bains dog – think I'm scared of you?'

'You're the one backing down now,' sneered Ranjit.

'Another day . . . another day . . .'

And with that the man turned and walked back to his car, got in and screeched off up Evington Lane.

Sukh waited until he had gone and got out of Ranjit's car. 'What the fuck was that all about?' he asked, looking at Manj.

'Don't worry about it – just some family business,' replied Manj. 'I'll tell you one day, Coz.'

The rest of the short journey home was made in

73

silence as Sukh wondered at what he had seen. As soon as he got in he went to ask his dad about what had happened.

Resham Bains hardly looked up from the television screen as he replied in Punjabi. 'You stay away from them idiots,' he said. 'That Tej is a drunk. Next time come home by yourself.'

'But Dad, what was going on——?'

'I told you – nothing for you— I'll call Ranjit's father later . . .'

And that was it. Sukh went up to his room and put his football kit in the wash. Just as he was about to get into the shower his mobile beeped a text alert at him. He picked it up and pressed the YES button. It was from Rani.

'AT NATS – COME ROUND – PLS? X'

He replied, saying he'd be there in forty minutes and got into the shower. It took five whole minutes for him to forget about his stupid cousins and think only of Rani . . .

 **RANI**

'What if I was bald and had hairs growing out of my nose?'

I looked at Sukh and wrinkled up my nose. 'Eeuurgh! That's nasty . . .'

'See — told you that you won't always love me,' he said, smiling.

I shoved him playfully. We were lying in his sister's bed during an afternoon off school. Not officially a day off or anything. We'd planned it. We should have been revising for our GCSEs, which were coming up fast, but neither of us had exams on our minds.

'Would you still love *me* if *I* was bald and had hairs coming out of *my* nose?' I replied, stroking his chest.

'You think there's a good chance that might happen?'

'No — but you know what I mean. I'm not always going to look like this . . .'

'I'll still love you when everything's droopy—'

'Now *there's* a lovely image. Do you really think that we'll still be together?'

'Nowhere else I'd rather be,' he replied, running his

fingers across my belly, making me wriggle.

'Yeah,' I said, thinking about something Nat had said, about men promising to do anything when they were lying next to you and you had no clothes on.

'I'm naked,' I continued, 'so you're not likely to say anything else, are you? I mean, you're not going to say, "Well actually, I think you're a dog and I can't stand you."'

Sukh pinched me somewhere rude.

'*Oww!* What was that for?'

'For being an idiot,' he said, laughing. 'I think you're wonderful, although in front of my mates you're just my "ting", innit.'

It was my turn to pinch him and I did, hard, on the inside of his hairy thigh.

'*Arrgh!*'

'Oh shut up, you ponce!'

'Yeah,' he said, in a silly, high-pitched accent. 'You's just mi gyal, man. You gets me?'

'You sound like one of them bad-boy wannabes from school,' I told him.

He leaned over and kissed me. 'Parvy's back over soon,' he said, changing the subject completely.

'Do you think she'll mind that we've been using her flat to . . . *y'know*?'

'Nah – I've already told her—'

'You've already *told* her? *Everything?*'

'Well, most of it . . .'

'Oh cheers, Sukh – I bet she thinks I'm a right slapper—'

'No she doesn't. She just told me to make sure that we were safe. She can't wait to meet you.'

'When's she coming back?'

'Couple of weeks, I think.'

'That soon?'

'Yeah – she's coming over for Mum's birthday. It's only for a few days . . .'

Secretly I was relieved that Sukh's sister was only coming back for a few days – I wanted to meet her and I was sure that I would like her, but at the same time the flat was like a different world that Sukh and I could escape to. I knew that it wasn't a 'real' world but it was still ours and I wanted to preserve it as much as I could. But thinking that way made me feel guilty and then I started feeling bad about myself. And Sukh noticed.

'What's up?' he said, as I tried not to look him in the eye.

'Nothing . . .'

'You sure?' he asked, doing this thing where he raises an eyebrow, something he does whenever he's genuinely concerned.

'Yeah . . . I think I'd better get going though . . . I need to meet Nat at her house.'

'Ten more minutes,' said Sukh, tracing an index finger gently down the bridge of my nose and over my lips.

I grabbed his hand and pulled it away, looking at him. 'So you'd still love me if I was old and grey and smelled?' I teased.

'Dunno 'bout the smelly bit. Nothing about being old that says you can't have a shower.'

'Good point – but you'd still love me . . . ?'

I looked right into his eyes and he didn't even flinch, holding my gaze as he spoke.

'No matter what happens – I'm always gonna love you.'

I took in what he'd said for a few moments and then I grinned. 'You know I'm taping this conversation. It's gonna be up for sale tomorrow – to all your mates. Imagine what they're gonna say about you and your soppy—'

Only I didn't finish because Sukh grinned and then bit me somewhere very rude . . .

I got in after eight that night and my mum was waiting for me. I put my bag down in the hallway and walked into the kitchen, which was split into two, a dining area and the main kitchen. My mum was sitting at the table, and when I walked in she gave me a filthy look.

'Where've you come from?' she asked in Punjabi, her tone stern.

'Natalie's,' I said without thinking. If I had thought about it I would have made up someone with a Punjabi name.

'Someone saw you in town today,' she said quietly.

My heart sank. I looked away and then back at my mum. My mind was racing. What was I going to say? I started to get really scared.

'*Well?*'

I walked over to the fridge, trying to stay cool and calm. 'I wasn't in town,' I lied, taking out a carton of apple juice.

'Someone saw you, Rani . . .'

I took a glass from the cupboard and poured myself a drink. 'They *can't* have,' I told her. 'I was at school and then I went to Natalie's. I even rang Dad to tell him.'

'So the person that said they saw you in town, with a *boy* – they were wrong, were they?'

I walked over to my mum and sat down. 'What do you *want* me to say?' I asked her. 'That I *was* in town when I *wasn't?*'

'I want you to tell me the truth,' replied my mum, looking me in the eye.

'I was at Nat's house. Why don't you ring her mum and ask?'

'She'll just take your side – you know what these *goreeh* women are like.'

I bit my lip to keep from shouting at her. 'Where's Dad?' I asked, looking away.

'In the living room.'

'Well go and ask him,' I said, my voice rising slightly.

'I'm asking you, and don't raise your voice to me—'

'Oh for f—'

My dad walked in and saved me from getting a slap. 'What are you talking about?' he asked my mum.

'Nothing . . .' she lied.

'Mum says that someone saw me in town today — with a boy,' I told him, hoping that he would take my side and get angry at whoever was spreading rumours about his little girl. My gamble worked because he was slightly drunk and he just snorted.

'They must have seen someone else's girl,' he said, 'because my girl was at her friend's house studying.'

'They were sure it was her . . .' continued my mum as my heart came close to giving way.

'*Who?*' asked my dad, raising his voice. 'You tell me who said that and I'll tear out her hair.'

'A woman from the *gurudwara*,' admitted my mum. 'She rang earlier. She was on the bus and saw Rani holding hands with a boy.'

'Is this true?' my dad asked me.

I gulped and then turned on the acting skills I had developed over the years to deal with my backward parents. 'Who you going to believe?' I asked. 'Some woman from the *gurudwara* or your own daughter?' I had tears in my eyes.

'*Beteh*, don't cry — it may just have been a mistake,' said my dad, putting his hand on my shoulder.

'*No!* It's just some interfering old hag! Causing trouble because she ain't got nothing better to do . . .'

My dad turned to my mum. 'See?' he said to her.

'You think that our girl would do such things? Don't you think she knows? If I ever found out that she was doing the dirty things that *goreeh* girls do, she knows that I would kill her and then kill myself.'

He was looking at me by the time he'd finished his sentence and my heart was beating really fast. I was scared of his threat because I knew that it was real. My fake tears were joined by real ones as I took in what he had said.

'Go on,' he said to me. 'Go to your room and wipe your face.'

I stood up.

'And remember – I believe you. But if I ever find out that you are lying . . .'

I looked right into his face.

'. . . I will throw you out into the streets like a dog.'

I turned and ran upstairs to my room, locking the door, still crying. Putting on a CD, really loud, I lay down on my bed. After two or three songs I picked up my mobile and rang Natalie, my dad's threat ringing in my head.

 **RANI**

I was excited, and apprehensive too, about meeting Sukh's sister. Parvy sounded like the kind of woman I wanted to be. Independent and successful. Not like a lot of Punjabi girls I knew who, like me, had to hide what they did under a veil of secrets and lies. Maybe it's a fault of mine, but I always hope that the new people I meet will like me. I go to great lengths to be nice to them, laugh at their jokes, smile brightly, that sort of thing. Usually this means that I don't end up being my real self, which is probably wrong of me. I'd told all of this to Sukh, hoping that he'd give me some pointers about his sister and what she was like, but Sukh just smiled and told me to be myself.

'She'll like you, Rani,' he said as we were walking through town to her flat.

She'd been back in the country for a few days and I was nervous as anything, what with trying to keep an eye out for snooping auntie-jis who might tell my mum that they'd seen me and attempting to put a brave face on my apprehension.

'How do you know she'll like me? What if she

doesn't think I'm good enough for you or something?' I said, as we ran across a busy road to avoid being mown down by a bus.

'I've told her all about you . . . she said – Watch the bus! – she said that you sound lovely.'

'Yeah, but she might not think that I'm lovely when we meet,' I moaned.

Sukh just ignored me and five minutes later we were standing outside Parvy's door. I'd been there countless times in the previous few months but that didn't help. I had butterflies and my mouth was dry. I was really nervous – so nervous that I felt like puking. Sukh got out his keys and started to unlock the door.

I followed him in, the nerves coming back even stronger. I mean, Parvy obviously meant a lot to Sukh and I'd never been in this kind of situation. The way he'd described her made her sound really great. I just hoped she would like me . . .

'In here, Sukh,' shouted his sister from the living room, where some R & B CD was playing.

We went through the door and Parvy stood up to greet us. She was tall and fair, with long, straight hair, and wore bootcut jeans, Nike trainers and a little red T-shirt with a henna motif. She was stunning. Instinctively I touched my face and straightened my clothes before smiling at her. She smiled back, her eyes studying my features.

'Parv – this is Rani,' introduced Sukh. 'Rani Sandhu.'
'Hi!' I said, all chirpy, likeable girl, smiling even

wider. I was doing it again. Please like me . . . please like me . . .

Parvy looked at Sukh and then at me and then back to her brother. 'What was your surname again, Rani?' she asked, in a friendly voice that disguised what a strange question it was.

I smiled back anyway. 'Sandhu,' I told her.

She looked at Sukh as though something was wrong. I straightened my clothes again. Touched my nose and hair. Was something wrong? Did I look silly? Had I said something wrong?

'Your old man – your dad – what does he do . . . ?' she asked gently.

I was puzzled now and just stared at her. What did my dad—?

'He owns a factory and some shops – hosiery and that, Parv,' Sukh interjected, replying for me.

Parvy sat down and swallowed. She looked at Sukh. Looked at me. Looked at her hands. Then she turned to me and tried to smile. But it just didn't happen. I felt like a child in the middle of a supermarket suddenly unsure of where her mum was. Lost. Confused.

'Bloody hell . . .' she said, looking at me.

'Parvy?' Sukh was glaring at his sister. 'Are you gonna tell us why you're acting so funny?'

I looked at them both and felt tears welling in my eyes. She didn't like me. I hadn't even had a chance to sit down and she didn't like me . . .

'I think I should go,' I said, close to tears. Why was

she being such a cow to me?

'No,' said Parvy, looking at me. 'It's not you, Rani – honestly. It's just . . .'

She looked away again and then asked me another strange question. 'Your family – they're from Moranwali originally, aren't they?'

I told her they were but wondered what that had to do with anything. I wanted to get out of her flat. Run away and never go back there again. I couldn't understand why she was—

'You better have a fucking good reason for upsetting Rani,' said Sukh to his sister, glaring at her.

'Please don't argue because of me,' I said feebly. 'I'll go . . .'

Parvy got up and walked over to me. She put a hand on my shoulder. 'I'm sorry,' she said. 'I don't know how to tell you this—'

'Tell us what, Parv?' asked Sukh, getting angry.

'I'm sorry but there is something you should both know,' she said, taking my hand and smiling again, only with a hint of sadness this time.

'Sit down,' she told me softly. 'This could take a while.'

MORANWALI, PUNJAB
EARLY 1960s

In a square of disused land to the south of the village of Moranwali, Mohinder Sandhu and Resham Bains stood by the weathered stone wall of a well, peering down into the darkness, telling each other stories as the burning sun fell in the sky like an orange disc and the late-afternoon breeze cooled their perspiring brows.

'There is a snake,' Resham told his best friend. 'Down there.'

Mohinder tried to peer harder into the gloom as if, by some magical twist of fate, the snake might appear from the depths.

'It is as long as a summer day and as black as night,' Resham continued.

Mohinder looked up at his friend. 'My father has told me all of this,' he said dismissively. After all, who didn't know about the snake? It was the talk of the village. Of the whole *shire*.

Resham looked annoyed. 'Did your father tell you that the snake appeared when the *goreh* first came with their red uniforms and their guns?'

'No,' admitted Mohinder.

'Well then, *bhai-ji* – shut up and listen to my story.'

Mohinder continued to look down into the darkness of the well shaft, wondering how long the snake might be if its length matched that of a summer's day. As long as him perhaps. As long as the road that led to Banga, the nearest town, maybe. And if it really was as black as night then how could anyone see it, down there in the gloom?

'The snake stayed after we threw the *engrezi* out of our land, to act as a warning to us to be good people.'

'And the people who do bad things fall down into the well?' asked Mohinder.

Resham swore at his friend. 'If you know the story, why did you let me tell it to you again?' he asked.

'Because you wanted to, *bhai-ji*,' answered Mohinder.

Resham peered into the void. 'Those who commit sins and steal and kill – they always seem to find their way to this place.'

'Is it some kind of *jaddu* – like magic?' wondered Mohinder aloud.

'Yes, *bhai*. You remember, last year, when Mohan Singh, from the next gully, ruined the *izzat* of Darshan Singh's wife.'

Mohinder smiled. '*Bhai*, I saw them out by the *gurudwara* – rutting like water buffalo. Darshan Singh's wife was bent over a plough—'

Resham cut his friend's recollection short. 'Well – they disappeared. No one knows what happened to them but it's obvious to me.'

90

'What?' asked Mohinder, already aware of the answer. It was a story that Resham told every time they came out to the disused well.

'They were *drawn* to the well. They fell in,' he said in a whisper.

'And the snake ate them?'

'*Ki pattah?*' said Resham. Who knows? In fact, who really knew if there was a snake down there at all?

'That's what my father tells me too,' confirmed Mohinder. 'So it must be true.'

The two friends stood for a while longer, peering down into the snake's lair, wondering if the well really was magic, and whether it really had taken the lives of Mohan Singh and that whore of a wife of Darshan Singh.

Mohinder and Resham made their way back to the village, along a dusty dirt track and through fields of corn, passing weary neighbours and friends along the way. The sun was low in the sky now and dusk beginning to fall. They passed a spinney, bordered on all sides by fields. A rustling sound came from the clump of trees, and then Kulwant Sandhu, the younger sister of Mohinder, emerged, her beautiful features disturbed, her eyes downcast as soon as she saw her brother and his friend.

'Kulwant – where have you come from?' asked Mohinder.

'*Bhai-ji* – I was delivering tea to our father, out in the

fields, and as I was returning to the village I saw something go into the trees,' she said, not looking up and therefore failing to see the longing in the eyes of Resham Bains as he gazed at her golden hair and milky skin.

'What did you see that made you go in there?' asked her brother, nodding towards the spinney.

'It was a bird,' lied Kulwant. 'It had injured its wing. But when I followed, it disappeared.'

Mohinder smiled and then took his youngest sister by the arm. 'You mustn't go into such places by yourself,' he told her. 'People have a habit of making up tales about young girls who do such things.'

'Yes, *bhai-ji*,' replied Kulwant. 'It won't happen again.'

'Come, favourite sister, let's walk home together,' suggested Mohinder.

Resham waited a moment for the brother and sister to walk on, enchanted by the way Kulwant's hips moved under her *salwaar*, so that her buttocks swayed slowly. The way her rounded and full breasts rose and fell under her *kameez*, with the lightness of her breathing. He felt a warming within himself and smiled. His friend's sister was the most beautiful girl in the village, truly an angel from Heaven. Even her voice, melodic and childlike, caused his heart to race. Perhaps when his time came, for he was still only sixteen, Resham's father would choose Kulwant Sandhu for him. After all, she was only a year younger than he, the same age as his brother, Billah. The possibility that they might marry Kulwant was the hope that kept many a young man in the village awake during the night.

In the midst of the trees Billah Bains watched his brother and Mohinder Sandhu walk on, leading his love home. He breathed easier now, the fear of being caught out with his beloved gone. He sat on a tree stump and put a hand to his chest, just over his heart, and heard it thumping as it pumped blood around his body. Racing away. He smiled to himself and began again the long, lonely vigil that he endured each time he was parted from her. Who knew if it was to be an hour, a day or a week before they touched each other again, felt each other's breath, smelled each other's scent. As he sat he realized that there was but one joy in parting from his *jaan*, his life, and that was the pure and overwhelming delight in rediscovering her touch, her taste, her smell.

He waited for a while longer, cooled by the soft breeze, before leaving his hiding place and heading for home. As he followed the path beaten a while earlier by his love, he looked up into the darkening sky, streaked as it was with bands of cobalt and midnight, and saw the stars begin to open their eyes and look down upon the Earth. He knew the star that he was looking for, had watched it every night as a child. It was his star, his guide, his light. And now it was theirs. His and his beloved's. A celestial charm which embodied their love and their passion and their fated union. As darkness chased the light of day away, he weaved and wandered his way home, entering the courtyard moments after his father.

'Where have you come from?' shouted Gulbir Bains, breaking into Billah's dreamy imaginings like a bullock through ears of corn.

'I fell asleep,' Billah told his father.

'Asleep? *Salaah bhen chord!* Are you man or a woman?' swore Gulbir, wondering what was wrong with his youngest son. What godforsaken affliction affected him that did not affect his brothers, Tarlochan, Juggy and Resham.

Later, as the family gathered to eat in the flickering light of oil lamps, and the moths fluttered and the insects buzzed, Billah sat by himself, barely touching the *saag* and *maakhi di roti* before him, dreaming of the day when he would be able to spend all his time with the girl he loved. As Billah sat and smiled to himself, his brother Resham wondered what was wrong with his younger sibling. Billah had been dead to the real world for a couple of months now, so distant and often wearing a look of bewilderment when spoken to. Always staring out at the Heavens as night fell and seemingly incapable of helping with the crops and animals. And very occasionally smiling to himself like a man possessed . . .

Kulwant looked up from her chores and saw the local priest walking towards her. Gianni-ji, as he was known throughout the village, smiled as he caught her eye, his short, stout frame weighed down by the mass that comes with healthy appetite and hours spent sitting, reciting stanzas first uttered by the gurus. An affable, constantly smiling man, Gianni-ji greeted Kulwant as if she were his own and placed a paternal hand on her head.

'My daughter, how are you?'

'I am well, Gianni-ji. And you?' replied Kulwant, taking a break from washing clothes at a pool used by some of the villagers to wash and by others as a watering hole for their water buffalo. Set amongst trees and high banks which shielded the rice paddies on the other side, the small waterhole afforded Kulwant a little privacy, alone with her thoughts.

'Daughter, what can I tell you? I am as well as my Lord allows and happy for that small blessing.'

'May you remain so for a long time, Gianni-ji,' smiled Kulwant.

The priest saw something in Kulwant's eyes. A feeling, a fleeting emotion. He studied her face so keenly that she found herself forced to look away. Realizing that he had embarrassed her, the priest too looked away for a brief moment.

'Tell me, daughter,' he said, 'does something trouble you?'

Kulwant looked to the ground. '*Nay, ji*,' she replied.

'Are you sure, my child?'

'Yes, Gianni-ji.'

'It is just that you seem troubled. As if your mind were weighed down by some great vexation.'

The priest looked once more into Kulwant's eyes, as a wasp buzzed against his turban. He swept it away with a flick of his wrist.

'I am only a child, Gianni-ji. What vexation could befall me at such a tender age?' asked Kulwant, unsure of the priest's intentions. Had he discovered her love? She shuddered at the thought.

'You are no longer a child, my daughter. Could it be that you are worried about something?'

'No, Gianni-ji,' answered Kulwant as sternly as respect for her elder would allow.

'I'm sorry, my child,' said the priest. 'Forgive me for being so direct.'

'No, no, Gianni-ji. Forgive me for speaking out of turn,' countered Kulwant, suddenly aware that she might have upset him.

'Whatever your reasons – just remember that I am here at your service. If ever there is something that troubles you, no matter what it may be, my door is as open to you as it is to your father.'

The priest smiled in his quiet, friendly way, and gave Kulwant a hug. 'God bless you, child. May you live a long life,' he said.

Kulwant smiled weakly, feigning renewed interest in her chores, as the priest went on his way to prayers. Careful to allow him time to walk out of sight, she then set down her washboard and block of soap and ran to the edge of the pool, retching from the very base of her stomach and expelling her breakfast. She retched again and then again before soothing her brow with a cupped handful of water. She sat back and sighed.

And then she began to cry.

Later, as she sat in the same spot, wondering if her family had missed her yet, she thought about Billah Bains, her love. Her lover. Would he pass by the watering hole that afternoon, on his way to help his father and brothers tend to their crops? The father for whom she would give her all to have as her own, so that she might take on the family name that she held as dear as her own life. The thought of not being wed to her love filled her with a dread, a fear so sharp that it bit into her during the night, as she lay and thought of her beloved. And during those long days when she could not find an excuse to go out to meet him; could not get away from the constant chores allocated her by her domineering mother and dumped upon her by her older sister, Preeto.

Occasionally, as now, she would sit and dream of being far removed from her family. Taken away somewhere distant and dreamlike by the man she called her life. A place where there were no chores to eat away the time that they could spend together. Where each moment was a lifetime long and her family could not dictate which of those moments she was allowed to spend with her love. Where they could lie at night, in each other's arms, and gaze at the celestial charm that Billah had claimed as their own. A dreamland that seemed so close when she touched his skin and felt his breath on her cheek. A place that was snatched away from them with every parting, every return to separate homes.

'Shall we tell them that we are in love?' Kulwant often asked Billah.

'One day,' he'd reply, 'I will approach your father and ask for you to be mine.'

'And he will agree with love in his heart.'

'Unless he discovers us too soon.'

Kulwant shuddered again at the thought of being discovered by her father or brothers. There were so many stories of ill-fated love, of lives destroyed by dishonoured fathers and raging brothers. Of lovers separated or forced into exile, beaten and murdered. Yet she felt a calmness when she considered her own love, fated by the stars. There was no one on Earth, either in her family or in his, who could part them from each other. There was only One who could achieve such a thing, and it was He and His stars that had brought them together. Why would He do such a thing – bring them together – only to tear them apart again? Calmed by her reasoning she stood up, walked over to the pile of clothes she had forgotten about and, picking them up, headed back to her father's house, each step taken slowly.

★ ★ ★

Being the youngest of a family of six children, and a girl, meant that Kulwant was forced to spend the better part of her evening seeing to the needs of the others. The job of feeding her father and four brothers belonged to the women, Kulwant, Preeto and their mother, Jagdev Sandhu. The male appetites of the Sandhu household were enormous, fuelled by the daily grind of farm life, and it was not unusual for each of the men to eat ten chapattis every night, with whichever seasonal vegetable or staple pulse had been prepared and, on the occasions when meat was cooked, two or three goats between them, over two nights.

Of her brothers only Mohinder paid Kulwant much attention, partly because there was only a year between them and three between Mohinder and the next sibling, Preeto, but also because Mohinder was a sensitive and happy young man. Jagdish, Kewal and Sohan were men rather than boys, each waiting to get married and dreaming of a new life in faraway England, the mother country, as their father Harbhajan called it. They had all three taken on the overbearing, tyrannical nature of their father and concerned themselves only with what they determined to be 'men's' affairs. That they had yet to find a husband for Preeto, who had reached nineteen years of age, was a cause of constant shame for the men of the Sandhu family, although they had recently exchanged betrothal pledges with a family from a nearby village so that this shameful state of affairs might be put in order.

Jagdish and Kewal were both due to be married later in the year, to sisters from the next village – brides who would spend at most a year with their husbands before the grooms emigrated to England for work. Sohan had also been promised a wife, a quiet girl from the same village, whose father was the local *sarpanch* or land sheriff, but he would wait a few years to follow his brothers overseas, remaining behind to tend the land while Jagdish and Kewal set up homes and lives in that faraway land. Kulwant's father Harbhajan was full of pride at the thought of his sons taking the family name overseas to set up a new line. It was the natural thing to do as far as he was concerned. The *engrezi* were calling for workers, the money to be made was good, and the rise in living standards would be a bonus. With Kulwant and her sister married off into new families, their parents could enjoy their old age flitting between India and England.

But as Kulwant lay awake that night, after finishing her chores for the day, she dreamed of a different fate for herself. An alternative life based on her own happiness rather than duty to her father or her family. A future with Billah. But how to broach the subject with her family? She could not go to her father or her brothers. Could not approach her mother or her sister. To say what? That she was already in love with a boy? That she was already the woman they had not wanted her to become until her wedding night? That was something she could never admit to – for fear of her life and that of her lover. Sometimes, as now, she felt as though she could curse the day that she noticed Billah for the first time. The day when they both turned fifteen, on that cold December morning eight months earlier. She did not curse the day, however, because to curse the day would be to curse her *kismet*, deny her fate. And in doing so would she not be denying her life, her *jaan*, too?

Instead she thought about Billah's eyes and the way he smiled. The way in which he had followed her to the waterhole days after their birthday and watched her do her chores. The way he hid and threw pebbles into the water, smiling as she tried to work out where they were coming from. The instant she looked into his eyes as he stepped from his hiding place and smiled at her. The feeling that her heart had taken flight right there and then, stolen away by the light-skinned, hazel-eyed boy who stood, grinning, before her. And then, as she fell softly into sleep, she felt that first touch, that first surrender to fate. A fate that would see her happy or see her dead. There *was* no in-between.

Resham Bains sat at the edge of the watering hole, keeping a close eye on his father's herd of water buffalo as they stood in the murky green water. Earlier in the year two calves had edged out further than they should have, towards the centre of the lake where the water was deeper, and drowned. Resham and Billah had tried in desperation to pull them away but the calves had panicked and begun to kick and flail, making rescue impossible. Indeed, had it not been for Resham's quick thinking, grabbing Billah's arm just in time, his brother's fate might have ended up mirroring that of the calves. Since that day Resham had carried a stout stick with him to the watering hole, ready to wade in to prevent any of the rest of the herd from wandering out too far. Not that he needed to. Perhaps, he thought to himself, these dumb beasts had more brains than they were given credit for, because they did not wander far at all, and often looked almost scared of the water.

The sun was high up in the bright blue sky and Resham felt hot enough to want to join the herd in the cooling water, put off by the layer of scum and flies that floated across the surface of the lake where it was unbroken. Instead he drank clean water from a small gourd that he had brought with him. Looking across the water to the opposite bank he saw Mohinder Sandhu waving to him. He stood and waved back, hoping that he could return the herd to the house and go and explore with his friend. A few days earlier they had found a disused hut out in the midst of some woods, well past any land owned by either family. Mohinder had told him that the hut was haunted; it had belonged to a witch who had died there. Being a *churayal*, he'd said, meant that she hadn't been cremated with God-fearing people in the sacred grounds, the *seveh*, but wrapped in cloth, burned without ceremony and dumped out in the woods as a feast for the wild animals. The stone hut had stood empty ever since but was visited every night by the ghost of the witch as she sought revenge against the men who had sent her to the spirit world without the proper formalities, leaving her soul to wander restlessly for eternity.

Mohinder, who came over and sat down by his friend, was holding a stick of his own. Thinner and longer than Resham's, it was the kind of thing you'd use to beat your way through dense undergrowth.

'What is that for, *bhai*?' asked Resham, already aware of what his friend's answer would be.

'It is to find our way back to that *churayal*'s house,' replied Mohinder.

'Let me take the herd back to our house first,' said Resham, gesturing with his head towards the water buffalo.

Mohinder nodded and smiled. 'Yes, and try not to let any of them drown today, *bhai*,' he teased.

'If you did any work,' Resham replied, after swearing at him, 'then perhaps you would know how difficult it is.'

'*Salahyah*, I do as much work as you,' countered an indignant Mohinder, cursing his friend.

'*Oh theery bhen dhi . . .*' swore Resham. 'I am only joking with you, *bhai*.'

Having returned the herd to his father's house, Resham didn't wait around for anyone to give him another chore. Instead, he refilled his gourd with water and, carrying it along with his stick, followed his friend out of the village, past the watering hole, through the copse of trees to the south and then out across the cornfields towards the woods. The path they had beaten a few days earlier had grown over already and they had to begin the process of finding the hut all over again. Careful not to step on any snakes that might be lingering in the dead leaves and wood on the ground, they pushed back the undergrowth with their sticks, sweltering in the humidity, their brows wet with perspiration and their shirts clinging. Mohinder led the way, trying to recall which route they had taken previously. Twice they thought they were close but twice they were proven wrong.

The humidity was increasing and they were beginning to tire as they smashed back branches and thick stalks, when all of a sudden they emerged into a clearing, the supposed witch's hut ahead of them. Exhausted, both boys fell to the ground and caught their breath. The air they were breathing felt as though it had been wrung from a hot, wet towel. Flies wriggled in the layer of sweat on their necks and their hair itched. Resham took his small gourd and offered it to his friend.

'Drink, *bhai*.'

Mohinder took the water and drank a small amount before handing it back. Standing up, he held out his hand to Resham, who accepted, and together they slowly edged towards the hut. The clearing was open but dimly lit, slivers of light breaking through the canopy above their heads. The effect was eerie, with the dimness broken by narrow beams of sunlight that a person might almost walk between. A forest of trees made of sunshine. In the midst of this forest stood the stone hut, dull and grey, and unlit. A rotting wooden door hung open, a gateway to the darkness within. And all around the friends, birds chattered, insects buzzed and leaves rustled.

'*Bhai*, I am scared,' admitted Mohinder.

'There is nothing to be *scared* of,' replied Resham with fake bravado. He was as frightened as his friend.

'If you are so brave then why are you standing next

to me and not going in?' asked Mohinder, clutching his stick tightly.

'*Chall feh*,' challenged Resham. 'Let's go inside.'

'*Nah, bhai* – after you.'

Resham looked at his friend and swore. Holding his stick like a truncheon at his side he moved through the forest of light and towards the hut. Somewhere amongst the real trees a twig snapped, an animal shrieked. Resham gave a start, gathering himself when he saw the smile on Mohinder's face, and repositioning his weapon in front of him. He took a step forwards and then another. An eagle's cry pierced the air.

This time Mohinder jumped. Resham gripped his stick and moved closer to the hut's entrance. Something at his feet made a gulping, warbling sound. Resham looked down in time to see a brown toad hop away into the darkness. He realized that there must be some water nearby. A well behind the hut perhaps, or maybe a stream. He edged closer, the smell of rotten wood assaulting his senses. From inside the hut he heard a soft sound like a gentle breeze through leaves. Dismissing it, he moved to the entrance and peered into the darkness of the hut. Mohinder came up by his side and did the same.

'Can you smell that?' Resham asked.

'Yes, *bhai*. It smells like something has died here,' replied Mohinder.

'The *churayal*,' said Resham. 'God knows how many things she killed here.'

Mohinder shuddered at the thought.

'I've smelled this before,' added Resham.

Something inside the hut made a sound – a mouse perhaps. A sort of sliding, scratching noise. Resham held out his stick, alert to any sudden movement. The noise stopped and then began again, this time accompanied by a gentle hissing.

'It's the smell of dead rats,' whispered Mohinder. He moved into the darkness a bit further.

Resham heard the scratching, sliding sound again. Whatever it was, it was moving nearer to them. He tried desperately to see in the darkness, but he could make out nothing. No shape that might belong to an animal or a person.

And then Mohinder moved further forward. A sudden silence was followed instantly by a sharp hiss. Resham, panicking, realizing what it was that lived in the dark, cool, dank hut, pulled his friend back with his left hand and swung the stick with his right. Mohinder cried out. Another hiss. And then a cracking sound, teeth on wood. Both boys fell backwards, Resham struggling to hold onto his weapon as something tried to pull it from his grasp. As he fell backwards and the stick caught a beam of light, he made out the powerful jaws and jet-black head of a cobra, its teeth embedded in the wood. He let go of the stick, throwing it back into the darkness, and sprang to his feet before pulling Mohinder up.

'*Bhai* – are you all right?' he asked Mohinder who,

although shaken and frightened, was fine.

'You saved my life, *bhai-ji*,' replied Mohinder, shaking.

'Never mind that now,' answered Resham, as he saw the giant head of the cobra emerge from the darkness. 'RUN!'

They sprinted from a standing start to the edge of the clearing, turning to see the irate cobra rearing up, ready to attack, its hood fanned out in anger, hissing and dangerous. They stood and watched it, thinking that they were safe, but suddenly the giant reptile, all eight black feet of it, sprang forward to the ground, heading in their direction. Resham turned and ran, tumbling headlong into the undergrowth, Mohinder crashing his own path through the vegetation right behind him. With no stick to smash a path through the plants and bushes, Resham stumbled and fell over a number of times as he tried to run, his legs catching against thorns and his feet slipping over dead roots and fallen branches. The humidity was closer still and he felt as though he was wading through water at times, but despite the burning in his legs and the thumping of the blood as it pumped through his veins, he managed to reach the edge of the trees, coming out into a cornfield. There was no sound behind him. No crashing through undergrowth, no breaking of twigs. Where was Mohinder?

He considered turning back to find his friend but he didn't. Mohinder knew the way back to the village and

Resham was sure he would be fine. Instead, he jogged round the edge of the field and past the copse of trees where Mohinder's sister had seen the injured bird, heading for the village. He heard a noise in among the trees of the copse, a panting shortness of breath. Mohinder, perhaps, hiding, trying to catch his wind. He walked into the clump of trees, heading towards the sound, ready to tease his friend for hiding. As he approached, the panting grew louder and then he saw them. Two naked bodies, male and female, entwined on the ground. A hip, a breast, bare buttocks and then the face. Her face. It was Kulwant Sandhu, Mohinder's youngest sister. Aware that he might be seen, he crouched behind a bush and tried to make out the man's face. As he watched, the man turned over and Kulwant sat astride him, her face contorted, his hands cupping her full breasts. Resham's heart started to beat faster and then it sank. He held back a cry of surprise and then stood up. Just before he could run away he looked into the eyes of both lovers. Right into Kulwant's eyes and right into the hazel eyes of his own brother. Billah.

Resham looked away in surprise and disgust and shame. And then he ran, hearing his brother calling after him but not stopping to reply. Not stopping for anything until he reached his father's house . . .

'You are my brother – please let me tell them myself.'

Billah pleaded with Resham in the early morning, hazy sunshine breaking through puffs of white, fluffy cloud. They hadn't spoken the night before. Resham had instead ignored his younger brother, unsure of what he should do. In the early light of dawn, the brothers had made their way out to the cornfields, as far from the rest of the family as was possible, in order to talk about what Resham had seen. What he wished he hadn't seen. He knew that what Billah was doing with Kulwant was wrong – it went against all the codes that had been impressed upon Resham from childhood.

And yet he could not pretend that he hadn't felt the same desires, the same impulses as Billah. And how could he betray his own brother, knowing that the Sandhus would be moved to injure him, at the very least, for defiling their youngest daughter? And then what would become of his fraternal relationship with Mohinder? He studied Billah's eyes, weary and red from a night without sleep, a night full of fear and worry. Eyes which were pleading for a chance to explain.

'Who will you tell?' asked Resham.

'*Bhai-ji*, I do not know who,' admitted Billah.

'Can there be anyone in the village who will not run to Kulwant's father at the first opportunity? You have taken her *izzat*, my brother. It is a thing that cannot be easily forgiven. You have cut off her father's nose.'

Billah looked to the ground and then mumbled about love and stars and marriage. But Resham did not let him off so easily.

'Marriage? Are you her *father* that you would settle her destiny for her? Can you not see where this will end, Billah?'

'*Bhai-ji*, we are in love. We want to be together . . . it was meant to be this way.'

'*Haraamzadah* – what will love do to help you when her father finds out? Have you never listened to the stories we have been told since we were children. Such affairs never end in happiness. Only in dishonour, sadness and death. And what of the shame to our own father?'

'I *will* marry her,' replied a steely-eyed Billah, his tone defiant, 'or I will die – understand that, *bhai-ji*.'

Resham saw it then – the determination, the passion that could have passed for a madness, there in his brother's eyes, burning hot like the sun. He flinched, not from his brother's words but from the intensity of his gaze. It was Resham's turn to look away.

'She is my life, *bhai-ji*. I will not settle for anyone else. If it means that we are to run away and be outcasts then so be it,' continued Billah.

'This is going to kill us all,' said Resham softly, shaking his head.

'Will you tell on us?' asked Billah.

'And see you *killed*? How can I? My own blood will be forfeit before such a thing could happen.'

'But what of your friend, Mohinder?'

Resham sighed as he looked at his brother. 'It will end our friendship, my brother. Of that you can be sure.'

'Even if we are married?' said Billah. 'For then we shall become brothers.'

'God willing such a thing may occur but do not count on it. The anger of a dishonoured father outweighs much, *bhai*.'

A sudden spark crossed Billah's face. 'Even the will of God?' he said quietly.

'What?'

'The will of God, *bhai-ji*.'

Resham shook his head. 'Are you insane, Billah?'

Billah didn't answer. Instead he told his brother that he had to see someone, and ignoring Resham's protests he made his way back to the village. Resham watched him leave and shook his head again. Deep inside he hoped against hope that his brother could save himself but there was a knowing, nagging feeling in Resham's head. It reminded him of past trysts that had been discovered; of violent murders and feuding families. There were things that were sacred in life and amongst the very highest was the *izzat* of a family name, the honour of chaste daughters. He had discovered his brother's affair. Soon enough someone else would too – someone who would not hesitate to inform Kulwant's family. And then all hell would break loose. It was as inevitable as the rising of the sun each morning. Hope was a fine idea, thought Resham, but it was like fool's gold where the dishonour of a *jat* Punjabi was concerned. What could Billah possibly do to make things right?

Kulwant was kneeling beside an irrigation channel that ran between two separate fields, using the cool water to soothe her brow and wipe the bile from her chin and mouth. Her stomach was in turmoil, turning over and over, and hard as a stone tablet to the touch. Each day she found holding down her food harder and harder. And now, with the sleeplessness brought on by discovery, it was harder still. She sat back and stared out into the field, wanting to disappear amongst the crops and the tall grasses; to find another world, safe and secure and far away from the trouble that she felt brewing. There was not only the unspeakable shame of being seen by Resham Bains, naked with her lover, but also the more serious problem of her family being told of her love. Ever since she was a child she had been told stories by her mother, stories which told of loose women and love affairs, of rape and dishonour. The very essence that Kulwant had surrendered to Billah was the key that she had been told of by her mother. A key that was only to be given on the chosen night of matrimony, to the only man who would ever have access to it. A man chosen for her by her father.

She thought of Billah's strong arms, calming her as she panicked, after they had been seen.

'He is my brother,' Billah had assured her. 'He will not betray me. Us.'

'But what if you are wrong, my love?' she had cried.

'Then we will run away together, Kulwant. Some-where far away where they cannot reach us or hurt us.'

'I'm scared,' she had told him, as he held her tightly.

'Don't be.'

'How can I not be? If my father finds out about us then he will *kill* you. I couldn't bear that.'

Billah looked away from her eyes for a moment, not wanting her to see the fleeting anxiety in his own.

'I could not *bear* it if you went before me,' continued Kulwant.

Billah smiled kindly. 'If I go before you,' he told her, caressing her naked belly, 'I will wait for you, up there in the night sky.'

'But how will I cope without you? How will I find you if I need you?'

'You will find me up there,' he said, pointing to the Heavens. 'At night. The brightest of all the stars.'

Nimmo walked over and held her palm to Kulwant's forehead. She stood with her hand in place for a while and then crouched beside Kulwant. 'You have slight fever, although I think that may be a reaction to being sick,' she told her.

'I can't hold my food down,' confided Kulwant.

Nimmo looked into Kulwant's eyes. 'Just when you eat or all the time, child?'

Kulwant looked away. 'Just when I eat,' she replied, lying. The nausea came on whether she had eaten or not.

Nimmo's eyes widened in surprise. She took her hand and held it at Kulwant's belly, prodding at it with her thick, calloused fingers. 'Sister, is there something I do not know?' she asked, her years of wisdom bringing her to a conclusion that she did not wish to come to.

'What do you mean?' asked Kulwant, not looking at her.

'You are like a tree in spring, Kulwant.'

'I don't understand . . .' replied Kulwant, beginning to cry.

'Blossoming, child. Tell me – did a thief break into your heart or did you give him the key?'

Kulwant gave a cry and grabbed hold of Nimmo, hugging her like a frightened child and weeping.

Nimmo shook her head and swallowed hard. 'Cry, sister, cry. Soon your father shall join you in your grief.'

Kulwant tried to pretend she didn't understand. Tried to pretend she didn't know what Nimmo was saying to her. But the old *chooreeh* made it clear.

'You are with child, sister. You have—'

'NO!' Kulwant tried to break free of Nimmo but was held even tighter.

'*Hai Rabbah* – what are we to do?' Nimmo asked of God.

'Please . . . don't tell my father . . . please,' pleaded Kulwant, finally resigned to the fate that she had silently known was about to befall her. It had taken Nimmo to make it real.

'Tell? Why would I tell your father, child? Do you think that I would welcome your dishonour? Your death?'

Kulwant blinked through the tears. 'My father would never . . .' she began.

Nimmo shook her head in sadness. 'My child, to your father you are already dead . . . believe me.'

Had anyone been in the vicinity of those fields they would have heard a wailing so loud, so plaintive, they might have presumed someone to have died.

Later, almost an hour after Nimmo had chanced upon Kulwant, the two of them still sat in the same spot, entwined like mother and daughter. Nimmo had been going over and over the choices in front of her. She could easily have left the girl to her own devices, her own fate, but that was something she could not bring herself to do. The poor, stupid, wretched girl had no inkling of the severity of her situation. There was death and dishonour to come, Nimmo could sense it. It was inevitable. And Nimmo would not leave Kulwant to face it alone.

There was the possibility of approaching Kulwant's family herself, but what chance did she, as a *chooreeh*, stand against the rage of a *jat*? No, such an option would bring only trouble for Nimmo, and her family. She would find herself accused of leading the poor girl astray, of being a witch and poisoning the girl's soul. There were poisons too, concoctions that she could give to Kulwant to take, which would flush from her the seed of her lover but take also the unborn child within. Yet such a thing could never occur without discovery, for the bleeding would tell a tale, and then there was also the question of God. Nimmo had no wish to go to her Maker with such a burden on her soul.

In the end there was only one solution. Nimmo would have to hide the girl away, let her family assume that she had disappeared, died maybe, or run away. Run away. Yes – that was the only thing for it. Nimmo would have to approach the girl's lover, break to him the consequences of his actions, and suggest that they go far away, to the city perhaps. Somewhere where they could not be found.

She rose from the ground and pulled Kulwant up to her side, telling her that she would take her to a safe place. Kulwant still wept, but the strength was gone now, and she felt as light as a feather in Nimmo's arms. As they walked, Nimmo asked her about her lover.

'What is the name of this thief to whom you gave the key to yourself, child?' she enquired.

Kulwant, weak and feverish, fought within herself. Why should she tell? Why should she . . . ?

'I must know,' argued Nimmo, 'so that I may approach him and tell him that you are undone. That you must, both of you, hurry away from here, before it is too late.'

Kulwant looked at her saviour and relented. After all, what was left to her now? What else could she do? The fate that had brought her to her *jaan* would be their only guide from now on . . .

'Billah,' she whispered weakly.

Nimmo heard the name and sighed to herself. Sandhu and Bains. Two large families, led by patriarchs who would have killed a man for laying even a finger upon their daughters. Two proud *jat* men, friends, both betrayed by their youngest offspring. There would be war. She sighed and continued to guide her charge to a place of safety, hoping that she could get to Billah before Kulwant was missed by her family.

Gianni-ji lit the sticks of incense and let them burn for a few moments before blowing on them, watching the flame pare down to a single glowing ember, the thick, sweet smoke swirling into the air and immediately filling the room with the scent of rose and jasmine. Repeating his prayer over and over, he sat back on a grass mat and let his mind wander, lost in thought. Later he would have to organize the *langar* at the *gurudwara*, the communal meal, but for now he was content to let his meditations take him away to the place where his mind met the words and the will of the Guru. Often he would stay locked in contemplation for almost an hour, unable to do anything else, oblivious to the outside world. But this morning was different. He heard footsteps making their way across the flagstone courtyard that stood to the side of the temple, the wooden door to his rooms creaked open and a voice called out to him.

'Gianni-ji, are you here?'

He opened his eyes and rose, his knees sounding like hinges that had been rusting for years. He offered a quick finishing prayer and then made his way from the inner sanctum of the *gurudwara*, through to his own rooms, and then out into the entrance, where he saw Billah Bains, his eyes red and swollen, his gaze lost somewhere between fear and resolve.

'Billah? What brings you here so early in the morning?' he asked the boy.

Billah looked down at his feet, unsure of how he would begin.

'Come, this is your house as much as it is mine. Sit.'

'Forgive me, Gianni-ji, for intruding on your prayers,' said Billah, sitting down.

The priest sat next to him. 'It is of no consequence, my child. God is always with us, whether we pray or not,' he assured Billah.

'I had nowhere else to go.'

The priest considered Billah's words for a moment before speaking. 'A serious thing indeed it must be if you cannot take it to your own father.'

'I am in trouble, Gianni-ji. I need your help.'

The priest nodded his head slowly. He stood up and put his hand on Billah's shoulder. 'Let me get you some tea, child. You look as though you have been fighting demons all night long.'

Billah nodded and sat back on the woven, wooden-framed *manjah*, his back resting against the sky-blue coloured plaster of the wall. The priest returned with two glasses of steaming tea, spiced with cardamoms, ginger and cloves, handing one to Billah, who blew on the tea's surface before sipping at it.

'Thank you, Gianni-ji,' he said, as the warming, spicy fluid relaxed him slightly.

'Now, what is it that you cannot tell your father?' asked the priest, sitting beside Billah once more.

'It is a matter that is very dear to my heart, Gianni-ji,' began Billah.

The priest smiled at him. 'An affair *of* the heart or just close to it?' he asked, wondering where he had seen Billah's haunted expression recently. On whom.

Billah looked away before answering. 'Of the heart,' he admitted.

'With a girl from the village?'

'Yes.'

The priest set down his glass of tea on the tiled floor. He stood and walked over to the door, shutting it. Turning to Billah, he ran his hand through his thick, long beard. 'And what is it you ask of me, child?' he asked, unsure of where the conversation was going.

Billah looked up at the priest, wondering whether he had made the right choice. Without averting his gaze, he changed the subject slightly. 'Tell me, Gianni-ji, is *love* something that God frowns upon?'

The priest was silent for a while, taken aback by the question. 'Well . . . um . . . no, I don't believe it is . . .'

'Then why is it that we, as men, frown upon it?' added Billah quickly.

'I'm not sure that we do,' answered the priest. 'The

love of our brothers is central to our religion.'

'And our sisters – what of them?'

'Our sisters too. But I believe that you are talking about a different kind of love. A love between one man and one woman.'

'Yes, Gianni-ji, I am,' said Billah.

'Tell me – who is it that you are in love with?'

Billah looked away again. 'Someone who is so pure and so beautiful that I cannot sleep when she is not there.'

The priest coughed and looked away too. If it had been possible to see the colour of his skin underneath his beard, it would have been red. 'What you speak of,' he began, 'is it a situation from which there is no turning back?'

Billah looked at him once more. 'Yes, Gianni-ji, it is.'

Billah expected the priest to shake his head, to curse him, to get angry. But the old man merely nodded and walked towards him, placing his hand on Billah's shoulder once again.

'My son, this is more difficult than you can imagine. Who is the girl of whom you speak?'

Billah felt a tear begin to fall down his cheek. 'Kulwant. Kulwant Sandhu,' he admitted.

'I see,' replied the priest, stroking his beard again.

'I know that we have done wrong,' said Billah, with tears in his eyes, 'but I wish to make it right, Gianni-ji.'

'You wish to marry this girl?' asked the priest.

'Yes.'

'And you require me to talk to her father?'

Billah nodded.

'This is difficult, my son. Our culture is such that a daughter's honour is sacred.'

'I cannot think of anything else to do,' cried Billah.

'You realize that I can talk to her father and to yours too, but that their reactions are not controlled by me?'

'Yes – I do. But you speak of culture, Gianni-ji. I know that it is not our way. But am I wrong in the eyes of God, to feel such a way?'

'As Sikhs we believe in marriage, my son. What you have done, it is hard to say if it is wrong. Sometimes these things cannot be controlled. Believe me, you are not the first one to talk to me of such things.'

'Really?'

'Yes, really. There are many things that happen that you youngsters are not party to. Love is a powerful feeling, Billah. But it is still a feeling given to us by our Lord.'

'So I am not wrong then?'

The priest shook his head. 'Whether you are right or wrong is between you and God, my son. It is not for other men to decide. Yet other men *will* judge you on this, and I fear that it will not be an easy verdict for you and that poor child,' he said.

'Will you speak to them for me? I do not wish them dishonour – I seek to become the brother of her brothers, her mother's son.'

The priest sighed at Billah's naiveté. 'Billah, it may

be too late. They will see your actions as a slight on their family name, on their *izzat*. It may be too much.'

'So we have no chance, Gianni-ji?'

The priest thought for a moment and then he sat down beside Billah. 'Tell me, who else knows of this affair, my son?'

'Just my brother, Resham,' replied Billah. 'And he will not tell anyone else.'

'So we could approach them without alluding to the real nature of your relationship with Kulwant?'

'That is what I was thinking,' admitted Billah. 'But are you prepared to lie to them for me?'

The priest smiled. 'I will not lie, my son. I will just not tell them about it.'

'That isn't the same thing, Gianni-ji?' asked Billah, confused.

'If my words can prevent a clash between your two families then I will be doing our village a great service. I have seen these things lead to bloodshed and death, my son.'

'So you will talk to them for me – for us?'

The priest sighed and then nodded his head before picking up his glass of tea and sipping from it. He looked at Billah with eyes of kindness and sympathy but inside he felt wary and unsure. He would appeal to both fathers. Talk of the greater love between God and man. Remind them that God would have no objection to such a union – regardless of any sin that had been committed. Any judgement was the preserve of the

Lord, not the duty of men. Yet he was not confident that it would do any good. There was much pride in both families and culture was almost stronger than religion in the village. He doubted whether his appeal would work, but at the same time he resolved to try, knowing that if he failed, there would be blood spilled in the dust and lives lost. And that was something he could not allow to happen without trying, at least, to stop it.

He sighed and sipped a little more tea before turning to Billah. 'Now, my son, tell me everything . . .'

As the priest stood and opened the doors once more, sunlight flooded into the room, bringing with it a new-found hope in Billah. It was as though he had unburdened himself of a great weight, something for which he was very grateful. He realized that there were no guarantees that his plan would succeed but it had to be worth a try, of that he was sure. Coming from the mouth of a man of God, surely his desire to marry Kulwant would be taken seriously. The priest coughed and told Billah to go home.

'I must speak to the *sarpanch* first,' said the priest.

The look on Billah's face must have told its own tale because the priest set about explaining why he had to consult the local land magistrate.

'Thekkar Singh is often called upon to settle disputes between two families, my son, and he knows your families well. Between us, I believe that we can find the right strategy with which to approach Kulwant's father, as well as your own.'

Billah nodded again. 'Thank you, Gianni-ji,' he said, aware that the old man was taking a great burden upon himself. He didn't *have* to do anything.

'It is my duty to bring peace where I can, Billah. My duty. Come back and meet me here later this afternoon.'

Billah stood up and headed for the sunshine of mid-morning. He looked out down the dirt track that led to the main part of the village, and smiled to himself. There was hope and renewed confidence in him as he set off for his father's house.

Billah spent the rest of the morning and early afternoon trying to concentrate on something other than his impending fate. First he made his way out to the fields to assist his brother Resham, who was tilling the land, telling him that everything was in hand. Resham asked Billah what he meant by this but he did not answer. Instead he took hold of the tiller and guided the buffalo bullock along its path, turning the topsoil evenly as he went, the toil showing in a slick, greasy layer of sweat across the water buffalo's back. Resham sighed and followed the plough, picking out any large stones or fragments that were lying on the surface and throwing them as far beyond the field's perimeter as he could. After an hour of silent work, the brothers stopped and took shade under a tree, drinking from their water gourd and resting for a while.

Resham looked at his brother. 'So, who did you speak to, Billah?' he asked.

'To the priest,' said Billah, realizing that he no longer needed to hide what was happening. Certainly not from his brother.

129

'Gianni-ji?'

'Yes – I told him everything, *bhai-ji*. *Everything*.'

Resham wondered how the priest had taken his brother's confession. Surely there was little that he could do to stop the affair somersaulting headlong into a feud between the two families. 'I am not sure that even the Gianni-ji can help you, Billah,' he said bluntly.

Billah shrugged. 'Then it is in the hands of our Lord,' he replied.

Resham looked out into the fields, past the panting water buffalo and the freshly turned furrows of earth. 'I hope so,' he said gently.

After noon had come and gone, the brothers headed back for the village, past a mound of drying dung patties that steamed in the oppressive heat and gave the air a smoked quality. These *phatta* would be used as fuel for fires once they had dried thoroughly, and there were always fresh supplies in the morning. The mound sat next to a piece of scrubland that had been left to wild hemp, the tall pungent plants adding to the smells of the village. Billah recalled chasing Kulwant through an entire field of hemp earlier in the summer, the foliage affording the lovers a degree of privacy that they had welcomed. He smiled as he led the bullock back to his father's house. Soon there would be no need for clandestine meetings and secret places. Soon the entire village would learn of the love between them. Hope began to burn afresh inside him and he could

130

hardly wait to return to the *gurudwara*, to hear what the priest had to say.

But wait is exactly what he had to do. Back at the house, Tarlochan, their eldest brother, made Resham and Billah clean out the hut that housed kindling for the fire and also doubled as a shed for the water buffalo when the weather was bad. Then they moved on to the feeding area for the herd, carrying iron buckets – bought from the travelling band of Romany that settled outside the village twice yearly – to the hand pump in the corner of the yard, returning with water to wash out the feeding trough. Straw, dung, dust and water were then swept away from the animals and collected by an open water channel that led from the yard out into the main sewerage channel and on into the cesspool. Once this task was done they washed themselves thoroughly at the hand pump, using bright-green soap and rags, before Billah, having dressed in clean clothes, made his way to the open kitchen area, where a pan of tea sat on the fire, simmering slowly, as his mother and Gian, his sister, prepared the evening meal of lentil *dhal* and fresh aubergine and *aloo*. Billah dipped a glass into the pan and then withdrew it, half full of spicy tea, which he blew on to cool it down. The strong, sweet aroma of thick cane sugar and creamy buffalo milk soothed him and began to quench his thirst even before he had taken a sip of the liquid.

He walked over to a *manjah* and sat down, wondering if he should make his way to the *gurudwara* yet. He stayed where he was for a few moments, drinking his tea, trying to work out what Kulwant's father's reaction would be. In his dreams he had often approached Harbhajan Sandhu and asked for Kulwant's hand in marriage. Each time his prospective father-in-law had smiled and hugged him, telling him that he would make as fine a son-in-law as there could be. But his dreams were his own and he had no inkling of the fate that Kulwant's father had in mind for her. There was no guarantee that the smiles and warmth of his nocturnal fantasies would become real. No guarantee at all. His only hope was the intervention of the Gianni-ji. Suddenly the tea stopped being a warming, calming beverage and became another obstacle to his future. What was he thinking of, sitting there, when his fate was in the hands of someone else?

He set aside his glass and stood up, his heart racing and his head beginning to pound as he headed for the *gurudwara*.

Nimmo found her quarry after two hours of searching the village and the land surrounding it. She would have found him sooner but she dared not ask the young man's whereabouts. It would have drawn attention to her and questions would have been asked. After all, what would an old *chooreeh* want of a young *jat*? Instead she had visited the cornfields and rice paddies of his father, taken a trip to the watering hole and the trees in the spinney beyond it, and wandered the narrow gullies and passages of the village, just in case he had joined the other idle *jat* boys, hiding in the lower caste quarters, smoking and making crude jokes well out of the earshot of their fathers. She had even walked out to the disused square of land by the old well, through the tall grasses and hemp plants, watching out for the spirit of the old *churayal*, which was said to reside in the heart of a particularly ferocious cobra. But she had not found him.

And then, as she toyed with the notion of asking for him, realizing that time was getting on, he had appeared like an angel, walking briskly along the dirt track that led to the *gurudwara*, his beautiful features set deep in thought, his eyes determined, resolute.

Nimmo let him get closer to her before she whispered to him. 'I have a message for you,' she said.

Billah looked at her with a mixture of pity and disgust. What message could the old woman possibly have for *him*? 'I have no time for your messages, Nimmo,' he told her.

She smiled, showing rotten yellow teeth, decayed after years of illness, brought on by the deprivation that was part and parcel of her lowly status in the village. 'You may have both the time *and* the need for my words, thief!' she spat, hoping to shake him from his apathy.

He glared at her. 'What! You dare call me thief? What are you talking about, Nimmo? Be gone, I've a very important task to attend to.'

'Yes, very important. If you are not to be undone, thief,' smiled Nimmo. Now she had his attention.

'Again you call me thief. Tell me – have I stolen anything from you?'

'Not me, Billah. But you have stolen.'

A terrible chill entered Billah's heart. For a moment he thought that the old woman knew of his real purpose, but then he shook the thought away. 'Get away from me, you hag!' he shouted. 'What do you know of my affairs?'

Nimmo ignored his raised voice and stepped in front of him, so that she was blocking his path. 'I know that you have stolen and I know that you are undone. Your key has unlocked something more than you imagined.'

Billah shook his head but did not move her from his path. Men did not raise hands to women, no matter what supposed station they held in life. Instead he lowered his voice. 'Nimmo, will you stop speaking in riddles and tell me what it is that you speak of – in the name of God?'

'Your tree is blossoming, child, as a flower in spring.'

Billah felt another icy sensation engulf his body. How could she . . . ?

'Now you begin to hear me, Billah,' said Nimmo, seeing the dawning of realization in his sparkling eyes.

'How—?' he began, before she shushed him.

'Not only have you stolen a father's honour—'

'How do you know of this?' demanded Billah, glaring at Nimmo.

'I have spoken to your love, Billah. I know every-thing. More than you even.'

Billah looked about them. They were alone. In a whisper he asked Nimmo what else she knew.

'You are to be a father — you who are not yet fully a man.'

'NO! It cannot be,' cried Billah, his heart sinking. Not because he did not wish a child to be born of his love for Kulwant, but because the news added a dangerous new twist to their fate.

'What did you think would happen? If you water your crops each day then they will ripen,' teased Nimmo, but only for a second or two. She could see the panic, the fear, rising in him.

He put his head in his hands. 'But I am truly undone,' he said with resignation.

'That you are, boy,' answered Nimmo. 'That you are.'

'You don't understand,' he told her. 'I have spoken to Gianni-ji — he is this very minute readying to talk to Kulwant's father, to ask for her hand on my behalf—'

Nimmo took the name of their Lord. 'Then we have no time,' she said.

'I must take Kulwant away from her father's house before he and Gianni-ji speak,' replied Billah.

Nimmo shook her head. 'Are you *so* slow of mind? How do you think that I know of all this?'

'I don't understand . . .'

'I have already hidden the poor girl from her family

– you must come with me! Now!'

Billah calmed himself and thought for a moment. 'Who else knows? Who else except you and me?'

'No one, Billah, but before the next full moon everyone will know and you will not be married before then. *You are undone!*'

Nimmo took his arm and tried to lead him. Was the young boy so stupid? Even if Harbhajan Sandhu accepted him as a husband, the family would know that Kulwant was pregnant before too long. It could not be hidden.

She tugged at his arm. 'Come, away!'

Billah looked to the Heavens. Is this what fate had in store for them – to run and hide like criminals?

'Come along, Billah. Your only hope is to run away – to the city – it is not safe here. They will realize she is missing at dusk. Hurry!'

Billah shook himself into action. The day was already beginning to seep away and the light fingers of dusk were appearing on the horizon. It would be dark very soon.

'You go to her,' he said, his voice showing newfound authority. 'I must get some belongings from my father's house. We cannot run without some supplies.'

'But there is no time—'

'I will be quick, Nimmo. I promise. Now hurry back to Kulwant and tell her that I will be along as soon as I can. We'll leave here this very night.'

Nimmo wanted to tell him that he had no time. That

136

they needed to leave that very moment, only she couldn't. She saw determination in his eyes. So she told him where Kulwant was hidden instead. As he walked away briskly, heading home, she turned and made her way back to Kulwant, praying that she had done the right thing. That the two young lovers would be able to get away and that her own involvement would not lead to trouble for her family. A father's rage was a terrible thing indeed.

Gianni-ji sat, cross-legged, in the *gurudwara* and prayed. Dusk was falling and there was still no sign of Billah. Although he had spoken to the *sarpanch*, Thekkar Singh, the priest had yet to speak to Kulwant's father. Now, as he waited, he prayed, hoping that he would be able to carry out his mission with the blessing of God. Even with such backing he knew that it would be difficult to control Harbhajan Sandhu's anger. Punjabi culture deemed that a father must protect his daughter's honour, no matter what. And though the priest had no intention of telling Harbhajan of the youngsters' affair, he felt sure that it would come to light. For what other reason would a priest approach a father in such a manner? Gianni-ji hoped that despite all of this, the girl's father would remain calm and see sense. It was a sensible match in many ways, the youngest children of two large *jat* clans bringing both families together. The Bains and the Sandhus were already well acquainted with one another. A marriage between Billah and Kulwant would merely cement that relationship. Make it stronger.

Finishing his prayer the priest stood slowly, his knees popping and creaking, and made his way to the side of the building where his cramped quarters were housed. He opened the stout wooden door and walked out into the courtyard. The sky was turning. Layers of teal and grey streaked the blue and the air was cooler all around him. It would be dark very soon and he had yet to speak to Billah. He sat down on a *manjah* and thought about the *sarpanch*'s response. Thekkar Singh had at first been taken aback by the news, unsettled, until the priest had reminded him of a similar situation that had involved Thekkar's own brother many years earlier.

'And you say that this is completely innocent?' the *sarpanch* had enquired.

'I did not say that, *bhai-ji*. By its very nature, this affair cannot be innocent. But it is not beyond repair.'

'I doubt Harbhajan Sandhu will see it so,' he'd replied.

'It is the only way to stop a feud, *bhai-ji*. The only way.'

The *sarpanch* had considered this for a long while before agreeing. 'In the interests of the village I will back your proposal. We cannot have feuding families here,' he'd said.

'It will bring the families together – rather than tear them apart.'

And so they had settled it. They had agreed to go to the girl's father together to suggest the union. They would tell him that the two youngsters had fallen for each other, that Billah wished only to do the right thing as a *jat*, and that they agreed with him. Surely, they would say to Kulwant's father, it is better to create a union between the two than to deny them? After all, both were the right age, the right caste, from similar families. It would be a solid union.

As he sat and waited the priest realized that his thoughts were repeating themselves, perhaps to reassure him about his intended actions. Whatever the reason, he was aware that Billah was late. There was very little time before darkness. He decided to give the boy a few more minutes. If he still hadn't arrived the priest would have to go and find him. Where *had* Billah got to?

'Are we destined to live as criminals then?' asked a resigned Kulwant, on hearing Nimmo's news.

'There is no other way,' said Nimmo, looking away. 'You are carrying a child and it will show itself in the roundness of your belly before too soon. There is no way that you will be married to Billah before that happens, even if your father *allows* you to marry him.'

Kulwant wanted to believe that Nimmo was wrong. She wanted to believe that there was a future for her and Billah in the village, among their families, a life lived in happiness and laughter. A life that did not mean running away to face an uncertain future in some far-off place. But she knew that she was hoping for a miracle. Nimmo was right. There was only one way out of the situation facing them – flight.

She looked at Nimmo and tried to smile, resigned to the journey that fate was unfolding in front of her. 'If that is what my *kismet* demands,' she said, 'then so be it.'

Nimmo put her arm around Kulwant and tried to reassure her. 'It is the will of the Lord,' she told her.

'Who are we to try to comprehend His ways?' replied Kulwant, tears beginning to fall.

'Hush, child, hush,' comforted Nimmo. 'At least you will have your love with you. Billah is a fine young man. He will not let you suffer.'

Kulwant wiped away her tears and buried her head in the old woman's shoulder, wishing that she could do so with her own mother – a mother who would be wondering where she had got to very soon.

'How long did Billah say he would be?' she asked Nimmo.

'He did not. He merely said that he would be quick and that you should prepare to leave tonight.'

'Then prepare I must,' said Kulwant, pulling away and getting up.

'It is growing dark,' warned Nimmo. 'Come, we must hurry – God willing, Billah is already on his way back here.'

Nimmo told Kulwant to wait and left the room, returning a few minutes later with a bundle rolled in cloth and tied with hemp rope. She handed it to Kulwant. 'It's not much,' she said. 'Just some clothes and a little money to help you along.'

Kulwant looked at Nimmo wide-eyed. 'No, I cannot take your money. You are too poor to be giving what little you have away,' she protested.

Nimmo smiled at her. A warm, loving smile. She shook her head. 'It is not very much, child,' she said. 'Enough to buy food for a few days. Take it and go with my blessing. I only wish that fate had smiled more kindly upon you both.'

'Thank you, Nimmo,' replied Kulwant, touched at the generosity of such a poor woman.

'Now, where has this man of yours got to?' said Nimmo, ignoring Kulwant's gratitude.

'I'm sure he will be here soon,' answered Kulwant. 'I'm sure . . .'

The last remnants of daylight were beginning to fade on the horizon as Gianni-ji made his way to the Sandhu household. He had given up waiting for Billah, assuming that the boy had been tied up on some errand with his father. It was the way of country life. Appointments were often missed due to unexpected situations – a missing water buffalo, a field fire and suchlike. Having already arranged to meet Thekkar Singh at the Sandhu residence at nightfall, the priest knew that he could afford to wait no longer. He would have to speak for Billah rather than let the boy ask Kulwant's father himself. Instead of his original plan, he had decided to ask Harbhajan Sandhu to go with him to the Bainses' house, in order that the two fathers might discuss the situation in the presence of the boy and reach a peaceful agreement.

The priest's eyes were old and beginning to fail, the edges of his peripheral vision becoming lost in a milky cloudiness, and as he walked, the path in front of him grew harder and harder to see clearly. In his haste he stumbled twice, catching his feet in potholes, but both times he stayed on his feet, more through the will of God than any sound judgement of his own. Ahead of him the village sat in darkness, apart from what seemed to be torchlight coming from behind a stone wall enclosure. As he approached another torch appeared to have been lit, followed by another and then another.

The priest entered the village proper and walked down the wide dust track that separated the *jat* houses from those of the *chooreh* and *chamarr*, the lower castes. A shout went up suddenly. And then another. Startled, the priest wondered what was happening, his fuzzy hearing unable to make out what was being said. And then out of the darkness emerged a group of men, who ran out from the low-slung wooden houses that made up the lower caste quarter, carrying burning torches which smoked and smelled of thick oil, shouting to the other residents.

'LOOK ABOUT! *DHEKKO JI!*' they shouted.

The priest called out to one of the men, Meni, asking him what all the fuss was about. Meni shook his head, as though gravely concerned about something.

'Gianni-ji,' he cried dramatically, 'there is villainy afoot!'

In the flicker of torchlight the priest could see the whites of Meni's eyes, the teeth missing from his mouth. He sighed. 'Meni – for the love of God tell me what it is. And try to do it calmly,' he told him.

'Hai, Gianni-ji – it is terrible. So terrible. A father is undone this night!' jabbered Meni excitedly and yet at the same time with an air of gravity.

The priest's heart nearly escaped out of his mouth. He looked away. 'Undone, you say?'

'Yes, Gianni-ji. Kulwant Sandhu is missing. She has not been seen since the morning.'

The priest's stomach somersaulted and his legs felt as though they were made of water. 'Where is Harbhajan Sandhu?' he asked hurriedly.

'We are going to his house now, Gianni-ji. To help him search the village,' replied Meni.

'*Satnam Waheguru!*' shouted the priest, calling out to God. 'I must speak to Harbhajan!'

'Come, let us go to him,' replied Meni.

The priest followed the crowd, the flames of torch and oil lamp throwing eerie shadows within the hazy bubble of light which floated around and above them all. The priest held onto his rosary beads, thumbing them at speed, each time offering a prayer to God, hoping that he was not too late to save Billah and Kulwant.

'*Ek Onkar, Satnam,*' he mumbled over and over to

himself as he approached the Sandhu family gully, where every Sandhu – uncles, cousins, fathers and brothers – had lived for three generations. The smell of burning oil assaulted his nose. A sense of foreboding turned his blood into ice water. Had Billah run away before he, the priest, could speak to Kulwant's father? Had he taken her with him? And what, he thought, as he heard the cries of Kulwant's mother and the curses of her father, had the *sarpanch* said to them, assuming he was already there?

Meni walked up to the priest. 'There is villainy here,' he said, almost as though he relished the tumult all around them. 'Mark my words, Gianni-ji. I saw this night in the clouds, in the omens, as the birds flew in circles this morning.'

The priest shook his head at Meni's superstitious nonsense, ready to tell him that God did not send omens in the clouds, nor in the erratic flight of winged animals. But then they turned a corner and found themselves at Harbhajan Sandhu's door, faced by the man himself, standing next to his four incensed sons. Harbhajan's face looked as though it had been carved from stone. Cold, emotionless, hard stone.

'Gianni-ji,' said Kulwant's father, almost in a whisper. A whisper full of menace. 'Tell me – why do you seek to cut off my nose . . . ?'

The Bainses' house was split into two sections on the lower level. Entering through a huge wooden gate, visitors would come into an open courtyard with a buffalo pen to one side and a water pump to the other, next to a stone outhouse. Beyond this, past two mango trees and a guava, was a covered area, one side a *rasoi*, where all the cooking was done, and the other an outdoor dining space. And past this point were four rooms, a stone stairwell to the first floor, and a side room that was often locked. It was locked because it contained valuable papers and Indian gold and rupees belonging to Billah's father, stored in an iron trunk.

Billah searched one of the other ground-floor rooms, trying to find a bunch of keys that he knew was somewhere around. He had seen his father put it away on many occasions but never in the same place twice. Gulbir Bains was by nature a cautious man, and he had heard many stories of bandits riding into villages and looting homes at gunpoint. Hence his concealment of the keys to his family's wealth. Billah had no idea where they might be but he knew the kind of places his father might put them and it was here that he was searching, all the while conscious of the fact that his family were outside, gathered by the *rasoi*, waiting to eat, as moths fluttered in the light of the oil lamps that were hung from the walls, throwing dancing shadows.

Billah knew, as he went about his business, that what he was trying to do was wrong. That stealing from his father would put the final nail in the coffin in which his reputation would be buried. Yet what choice did he have? His father would be able to make the money back quickly enough, but what good was Billah to Kulwant if they ran away with nothing but the clothes on their backs? Sure in his own mind that God would forgive him, he continued to search, grimly aware that he had very little time left before he would have to make his escape with Kulwant. Darkness had fallen and he knew that Kulwant's family would by now be looking for her, angry and vengeful in their mood. He was wondering whether the priest had spoken to Harbhajan Sandhu when he heard his father call to him. He considered ignoring him but quickly realized that it would do no good. His brothers had seen him enter the room and there was only one exit. Instead he resigned himself to escaping without any money at all, and he left the dark, musty room, telling himself that his fate was now in the hands of God. If this was His design for both Billah and Kulwant, then so be it.

'What were you doing in there?' asked his father, eyeing him suspiciously.

'Nothing,' replied Billah. 'Just looking for something.'

'Well, forget whatever it is and sit down with your father and brothers like a man,' said Gulbir Bains, wondering when his wayward son would grow up.

Billah told him that he wanted to speak to his mother and walked over to where she sat on her haunches with Gian, rolling out and baking chapattis.

'Are you well, my son?' asked his mother, as he crouched down next to her.

'Yes, Mother – why do you ask?' he said, smiling, hiding the pain that he was beginning to feel deep inside at the thought of leaving his family, particularly his mother and sister, under such circumstances.

His mother wiped a flour-covered hand on her clothing and then stroked his cheek with the outside of her hand. 'You look as though you have seen a ghost,' she told him with maternal concern.

'I'm well, *maa-ji*. May God bless you.'

His mother gave him a quizzical look, wondering what he was getting at. But she let it go, putting it down to the changes that his adolescent mind seemed to have been going through recently. Instead she smiled at him. 'You know that, even as a man, you can tell me if something is wrong?'

'*Han-ji*,' he replied, 'I know. I will always love you, Mother.'

This time his sister gave him a strange look, and then turned to their mother. '*Maa-ji*, I think my brother has been touched by some black magic,' she said, teasing

148

Billah with her laughter.

Their mother shrugged it off. Her son had always been a little strange – from making up little songs as a two-year-old to crying the first time he saw his father beat a lazy buffalo. She put it down to the Will of God and left it at that.

Billah was busy rubbing flour into his sister's face when she told him to stop. 'You don't do that to your elders,' she scolded him playfully. 'Idiot. Go and sit by your brothers . . .'

Billah put his arms around her. 'May you live for ever, *maa-ji*,' he said to her, his unguarded show of affection catching her by surprise.

She laughed. '*Dhuffa Hor*, idiot!' she managed to say despite her laughter. 'Go and sit down. Your food will be ready soon.'

Billah got up and walked over to his brothers, quickly wiping a single tear from his eye, hoping that he had not been seen, as a huge well of emotion threatened to engulf him. He would never see his mother again once he left the house, he knew that. Nor his sister, nor Resham, nor his older brothers. Disavowed by his father and left to fend for himself, Kulwant and their child. He cursed his *kismet* for forcing him down such a path before sitting down beside Resham, working up to the point when he would find an excuse to go outside and never return.

Gianni-ji stood with his head held high, his eyes

burning into those of Harbhajan Sandhu. The *sarpanch* had beaten the priest to Kulwant's father and told him of Billah's request. As expected the father's rage had overcome his rationality and he had become abusive, casting doubt over the legitimacy of Billah's grand-father and calling his mother a whore. The *sarpanch* had tried to calm him down but he had refused to believe that the affair was an innocent one, calling for his sons to go and find the Bains boy and avenge their sister's honour with blood.

And then Kulwant had not returned from her chores. As dusk had given way to the pitch darkness of night, Kulwant's mother had become hysterical and her father even more livid. A huge cry had gone up in the village to help find Kulwant, and Harbhajan had demanded to see the priest. Gianni-ji had duly obliged. Now they were standing face to face, as two bulls would, ready to fight over a herd of cows. Gianni-ji was desperately trying to calm Harbhajan but it was all in vain.

'If you were not a man of God, Gianni-ji, I would separate your lying tongue from your mouth with my own hands,' shouted Harbhajan, as they stood in the Sandhus' courtyard surrounded by other men from the village.

'Your words hurt me grievously, Harbhajan, but you must try to understand—' started the priest for the fourth time, only to be cut off by Kulwant's father once more.

'Understand? If you had a daughter you would know how heavy the burden is that a father must carry!'

'She has done nothing wrong,' lied the priest, hoping that God would forgive him.

'That is what you say, but I tell you that I know it to be different! Where is this boy who asks for my daughter's hand and then kidnaps her away?'

'We do not know that he has,' said the *sarpanch* sternly, asserting his authority in the village pecking order, such as it was.

'You and this supposed man of God may say what you like,' shouted Harbhajan, 'but I will not be denied.'

'Mind your words, *bhai*,' answered the priest, suddenly angry. 'You have not the first idea of what it means to be a Sikh.'

'Is this shameful deceit what it means?' demanded Harbhajan.

The priest shook his head in sadness. 'The shameful deceit is yours, Harbhajan. You, who call yourself *Singh* but know nothing of your supposed religion.'

'And what do you mean by that?!' raged Harbhajan.

'Even if they have done wrong, *bhai-ji*, it is not for us to judge them. That is the domain of our Lord,' answered the priest, immediately sorry that he had spoken.

'So you admit it at last!' cried Harbhajan Sandhu. 'The boy has stolen my daughter's *izzat* and yet still you support him!'

'That is not what was said,' interrupted the *sarpanch*, aware that the situation was poised at a crossroads and about to take a bloody turn if left unchecked.

'Enough of your lies!' shouted Harbhajan Sandhu.

He called for his sons to fetch weapons and, barging both the *sarpanch* and the priest to the ground, he set off for the Bainses' house with his sons, an ever-growing mob of village men behind them carrying lanterns, oil lamps and burning torches of flame.

The priest called out to the mob, begging them to stay calm, but any reason that they might have had was gone, replaced by the pack mentality that often left the priest wondering whether men really were any different to beasts. Taking the helping hand offered by the *sarpanch*, Gianni-ji got slowly to his feet and dusted himself off, before the two of them set off after the mob, still hoping that they could make Harbhajan Sandhu see sense.

A chorus of shouts echoed through the blue-black night, followed by another and then another.

'Nimmo – what is that shouting?' asked Kulwant, trying to make it out.

'I do not know, child. Let me go out into the street and find out. Wait here.'

Nimmo opened the door slowly, peering out to make sure that no one was watching. Edging through slowly she shut it behind her and turned the rusting key in the lock. Two doors down a neighbour came out carrying a flame torch. Nimmo walked over to him. '*Bhai-ji*, what is happening?' she asked, as the acrid smoke from the torch made her eyes water.

'They are looking for someone,' said the neighbour.

Nimmo's heart turned to water. '*Bhai-ji*, who is it that they seek . . . ?' she asked tentatively.

'Kulwant Sandhu, daughter of Harbhajan Singh Sandhu, from the far gully. She has not come home. They say that she has been taken away by a man – her *izzat* at her feet, her father's turban at his,' replied the neighbour, shaking his head as though he were full of woe.

'Do they know who it is – this thief?' asked Nimmo, feeling queasy.

'The boy with the *billeh* eyes. Billah Bains. Harbhajan Sandhu is going there now to find him.'

With that the neighbour walked briskly towards the commotion along with others. Nimmo felt a dark cloud cover her soul. She had broken into a sweat, her heart racing. Turning back she hurriedly opened the door to Kulwant's hiding place, an old hut which had belonged to Nimmo's own father and had been deserted for years.

Kulwant looked at her as she entered, sensing the change in her mood, the look of fear in her eyes. 'What is it, Nimmo?' she asked.

'It is grave news, child. Your father is on his way to Billah's father's house, ready to kill your love.'

'*Hai Rabbah!*' cried Kulwant, raising her hands to the

Heavens. 'What fate is this, Lord?'

'Hush, child, you will be heard,' whispered Nimmo, but Kulwant ignored her, wailing and crying and cursing her *kismet*.

'We do not even know whether he is still there,' Nimmo told her. 'He may be on his way here at this very moment—'

'But what if he has been caught by my father?' cried Kulwant. 'How will I know . . . ?'

Nimmo sighed. She would have to do one more thing for the poor children. 'Wait here – quietly! I will be back when I have some news,' she said.

Kulwant nodded, unable to speak because her stomach was turning somersaults and her mouth was suddenly parched. Nimmo left the hut and locked the door behind her, peering into the darkness, as she made her way to the Bainses' house. The sinking feeling in her bones told her that fate was not on the side of the lovers that night . . .

Gulbir Bains heard the mob first. He stood quickly and picked up his cudgel, a stout, hardened staff of wood that was almost black, before walking to the main gate, past the nonchalant water buffalo, their eyes shining luminously in the dark. His sons, Tarlochan, Juggy and Resham, stood and followed him but Billah, a feeling of dread encompassing his mind, stayed where he was. His mother came running, asking him what was wrong, outside in the darkness. Billah shrugged his shoulders and told her he didn't know. Instead he looked around for an escape route, realizing that he would have to go up onto the first floor and jump onto the neighbour's roof, which was almost adjoining. He stood and edged towards the stone stairwell, his heart beating, mind racing.

Gulbir Bains was at the wooden gate, unlocking it, unaware that the mob were baying for his youngest son's blood. He merely assumed that it was some village crisis that was causing the fuss, an attack by bandits perhaps or an unexplained death. Eager to find out, he snapped the padlock open, wound out the thick iron chain and pulled the gate back, torch flame lighting his face. The mob was forty strong outside, headed by Harbhajan Sandhu and his sons. Gulbir opened his mouth to speak but never got his words out, a cudgel swinging through the darkness and splitting his head open. He crumpled to the ground, hearing the shouting erupt all around him but unable to see what was going on.

Had he been able to watch he would have seen the horrified reaction of his own sons, the cries, the curses, and then the storming of his home by the mob, Harbhajan Sandhu leading the throng. He would have seen the men of the village, his own friends, grab hold of his three eldest sons and hold them back as Harbhajan's sons, Jagdish, Kewal and Sohan, ran to catch Billah, who had by this point scampered up the stairwell in a bid to escape. But by that point Gulbir had passed out, blood streaming from the head wound inflicted by Harbhajan Sandhu.

Billah was dragged back down the stairwell by Kulwant's brothers and held in front of the mob, as Harbhajan Sandhu screamed obscenities at him. In his peripheral vision he saw his poor mother, wailing and crying and trying to reach him, asking over and over, 'Have mercy, *bhai-ji*! What has my boy done?'

But Kulwant's father ignored her pleas and spoke to the assembled crowd instead. 'Here he is – this thief. The one who has taken my daughter and my *izzat*. This dog who thought he could cut off my nose!'

Some of the onlookers shook their heads, some called him names and a few prayed out loud that there would be no more bloodshed that day.

The priest stepped forward and stood between Harbhajan and Billah, pleading. 'Harbhajan – this is not the way of our Lord – *listen* to me . . .' he cried, only to be ignored and then beaten down by Harbhajan's cudgel.

A huge collective sigh of shock and horror went up, as some of the crowd stepped away. Harbhajan Sandhu had raised his hand to Gianni-ji. He might as well have raised it to one of the *panj piarah* or the gurus them-selves. The priest fell to the ground, his head in his hands, and then the *sarpanch* stepped forward, his eyes blazing.

'No matter what wrong has been done you, Sandhu-ji,' he told Harbhajan, 'you have done more wrong yourself. You will pay for your actions, mark my words.'

But rage and intemperance had hold of the wronged father and his sons, and the words of the land magistrate, normally imbued with the full force of the law, were cast aside. There was no place for laws where a father's *izzat* was concerned. Such things were only dealt with in one way.

'You dare to tell me how to deal with such shame?!' shouted Harbhajan.

'Mercy!' came a cry from Billah's mother.

'You whore!' spat Harbhajan. 'Were it your daughter

and another's son you would be barking for blood as a bitch barks for food.'

Billah's brothers struggled to break free on hearing their mother slighted, already enraged at the attack on their father. Murderous intent clouded their vision. Harbhajan Sandhu pushed the *sarpanch* aside too and took hold of Billah, whose hands had already been tied by Kulwant's brothers, dragging him out of the house and into the village so that all could be witness to his wrongdoing. As he dragged him along, Harbhajan Sandhu called out for all to come and see.

'Look now, all who are men! Look at this thief – this son of a rabid whore who has polluted my name and dragged my *izzat* through the mud as if it were nothing. Look how he pays . . .'

Had Gulbir Bains been able to watch he would have seen his youngest child dragged to the square in the middle of the village, followed by his brothers and his distraught mother. He would have seen the look of fear in his youngest child's eyes as people who were friends and colleagues, and even relations, spat at him and called him names. He would have heard Harbhajan Sandhu demand to know what Billah had done with Kulwant – where he had taken her. And he would have seen Billah shake his head, tell Kulwant's father that he bore him no malice, and explain that he only had to answer to his Lord – not to mortal men with cudgels and blades. He would then have seen Harbhajan Sandhu, his old friend, drive a long, pointed blade through Billah's chest and out of his back, heard the screams of his wife and daughter, the cries of horror from the mob, now shamed by their bloodlust; and then, as his youngest child lay dying in the dust, Gulbir would have heard him call out to his Lord, ask for forgiveness and, with his last breath, declare undying love for Kulwant Sandhu . . .

From the shadows, Nimmo watched Billah die, tears streaming down her face. She watched the priest kneel in front of the dead boy and hold his hands up to the Heavens. As she turned and ran she heard the Gianni-ji call out.

'My Lord – how did such hatred come from love? Tell me, O Lord – what villainy is this?'

LEICESTER

 # RANI

There were tears falling down my cheeks as Parvy finished telling us the story. I had hold of Sukh's hand and, looking down at it, I realized that I had squeezed it so hard, his fingers had gone almost white. I let go and wiped away the tears but they were soon replaced by more. Parvy looked at her brother then got up and came over, crouching in front of me. I didn't know what to think or do. It was such a shock. How come I'd never heard the story from my own family? I didn't even know that I had another aunt. And then I realized that my father would never have told me about it – it undermined all his lectures about filthy white girls . . . But surely someone in my family . . . my brothers . . . ?

'It's OK,' Parvy told me, putting her hands on my knees.

'Why didn't I know about all of this already?' I asked her, trying really hard not to cry. And failing.

'I don't know,' Parvy told me. 'I really don't know.'

Sukh stood up and started pacing the room. No one spoke for a few minutes before he broke the silence.

'This is so messed up, man. I didn't know any of this
– none of it,' he told me.

'Our families have had this thing going on for years,'
said Parvy. 'Dad thought that it was all over – and he
didn't want you to know. He wanted you to grow up
without having to deal with the same stuff he had to –
all the shame and the sadness and stuff. I only found
out because I walked in on an argument, back when
you were about six. He sometimes talks about Rani's
dad, Mohinder – they were good friends once.'

'I kinda *thought* Rani's name rang a bell when we
met but I put it out of my mind. I thought that I was
just being stupid . . . And now I find out there's a
feud . . .' said Sukh, talking to his sister but looking at
me.

'Yeah – although it's been years since anything
major happened between our families. Some of the
younger idiots kick off now and then – but they just
use it as an excuse for fighting and acting like animals.'

I looked at Sukh and then at Parvy. I was confused.
How could I not have known? How could my family
not have told me? 'So your uncle, Billah, was killed?' I
asked.

'Yeah.'

'What happened to my aunt? Something must have
happened because until just now I didn't even know
about her.'

Parvy looked away. 'She killed herself – jumped in a
well, I think. No one really knows because they never

164

found her body. Just her shawl – lying next to the well.'

'But she was . . .' I began.

Parvy put her hand on mine and squeezed. 'I know, I know . . .' she said.

'Oh, this is horrible!' I shouted suddenly, and then wished that I hadn't. But what was I supposed to do? I didn't know what to think. My family hated Sukh's family, and there we both were, seeing each other.

Parvy stood up and walked over to the window. She started to speak but stopped and thought for a while. Then she went on, 'Our family had to leave the village after Billah died and Kulwant vanished. The elders thought it would be the best way to stop any more blood being spilt. But the feud continued. Both our fathers moved to Leicester in the nineteen sixties and there've been incidents between them, off and on, over the years . . .'

I shuddered. My mind was going in about a million directions at the same time and I felt numb. Sukh tried to take hold of my hand but I pushed him away. I didn't want to – it just happened that way. I couldn't control it.

Parvy turned and looked at me. 'There've been fights between our uncles, our cousins – we even go to separate *gurudwara*. It's been calm for a few years now though.'

'But it just doesn't make any sense,' I told her. 'How could me and Sukh not have known about it?'

'I dunno how someone didn't let it slip.' Parvy

shrugged. 'But I'm sure Dad told everyone not to tell you about it, Sukh. When I found out he told me never to mention it again. He said that it was like cutting open an old wound . . .'

Sukh just sat where he was, looking from me to Parvy and feeling a little hurt at my rejection, I think. I just didn't want to be there. Didn't want to be around them. I needed to think . . . I needed to call Nat. I needed to cry again too.

Something in my head snapped and I shot up from my seat. 'Gotta go,' I mumbled, not looking at Sukh or Parvy. I headed for the door.

'Rani . . . wait,' said Sukh, coming after me, but I didn't wait.

I ran to the door, threw it open and went out into the corridor. I rushed down the stairs and out into the street, the glass door to the foyer slamming shut behind me. I looked up, tears blurring my sight, made out a taxi and ran to it, got in and told the driver to go. As he pulled away I saw Sukh standing across the street from me, shouting. I think he was still telling me to wait. I don't know. I didn't want to talk to him, didn't want to touch him. Just wanted to go home. Just wanted to . . .

 **SUKH**

Three days after Parvy had told him and Rani about the feud, Sukh sat on his bed with some R & B thing playing on his CD. He wasn't listening to it. He was sitting thinking, watching the signal light on his mobile flash on. And off. And on. And off. Rani hadn't answered her phone since she'd run out of Parvy's flat. Sukh had only heard from her once. She'd sent a text telling him that she didn't want to talk to him. Her phone had gone straight to answer every time he'd tried calling. Each of the thirty or forty times. And she wasn't replying to his text messages either. He'd just sent the latest one and was sitting staring at his phone, willing the message tone to bleep at him and put him out of his misery; imagining her face in his mind, thinking about her touch and her smell and the way she tasted when he kissed her.

His family wasn't really talking to him. He'd returned from Parvy's flat angry and sullen and had told his dad to fuck off. His dad had reacted with measured calm, not slapping him or swearing back – just walking away, shaking his head. That had been

167

three days ago and since then only his mum had tried speaking to him, in vain. Sukh wasn't in the mood to talk to anyone. Not his parents, nor Parvy and definitely not his mates. Jaspal had sent him loads of messages and rung three times each day but Sukh had ignored him. He couldn't think of anything but Rani. He wasn't hungry, he couldn't sleep. He didn't care what time it was. He just wanted Rani to call or send him a text to say that he should meet up with her. Hold her hand. Make her laugh. Like it was before he'd taken her to meet Parvy and ruined it all. Like it was before . . .

The mobile bleeped three times in quick succession and Sukh's heart jumped into his mouth. He grabbed the thing and pressed the READ NEW MESSAGE button. His heart went back to where it had come from. Jaspal. Sukh deleted the message without reading it and threw the phone back down on the bed. The CD finished and he leaned over to where the player sat and started it again, the thump of the bass not getting him going like it usually did. He got up off his bed and paced his room, usually so tidy but looking now like someone had played a bhangra gig in it. He paced for about five minutes, all the while looking at his mobile and turning it round in his hand as the signal light flashed on. And off. And on. And then he sat back down.

Ten minutes passed as Sukh sat and stared at the wall, then he picked up his phone again and scrolled through the menu to WRITE MESSAGE. He looked at the small screen for a moment and then began to type in another message.

PLS LET ME NO THAT U R OK. CALL ME PLS. LOV U.

For the next twenty minutes Sukh went through the same routine, sitting on his bed, pacing his room and thinking about Rani. The signal light flashed on and off but there were no bleeps from his phone. He tried again.

PLS CAL ME. I LOV U. JUST WANNA TALK. CANT SLEEP. PLS RANI.

When he realized that Rani wasn't going to reply, no matter how many times he sent her messages, Sukh got angry and threw his phone on the floor, grabbed his jacket and stormed out of his bedroom, downstairs and into the street, not knowing where he was going . . .

 **RANI**

'Just call him.'

Nearly a week after I'd run out of Parvy's flat I was watching the rain fall outside my bedroom window, holding my mobile to my ear and trying to listen to Natalie.

I hadn't spoken to or seen Sukh for all that time and it was killing me. But I didn't know how to sort out the mess that I had created when I ran away. When I had sent him that text, telling him that I didn't want to talk to him: I had been angry, upset. I hadn't meant never again . . .

And now I didn't know if *he* would want to talk to me. I hadn't had any messages in the last couple of days. What if he was angry? What if he wanted to drop me? And what was I supposed to say? Hey Sukh, sorry for being so rubbish but I'm back now and I'm OK about it all . . . ?

'Are you listening to me?' asked Nat.

'Yeah I'm listening,' I told her.

'You've got to *hear* me too, babe,' she replied, sounding a bit exasperated.

'I'm sorry, Nat.'

'That's what you need to tell Sukh too,' she said.

'He'll just tell me to get lost.'

'No he won't.'

'How do *you* know?'

'Let me think . . .' she began.

'I didn't reply to any of his messages, Nat, and now he's stopped sending them. He'll probably drop me like a stone . . .'

She sighed for about the tenth time since I'd called her. 'Look – do you love him?' she asked.

'More than anything . . .'

'And you're OK with this whole feud thing?'

I grinned despite myself. 'It is a bit Bollywood—' I began, but Nat cut me off.

'Answer the question, minx.'

'Yes – I'm fine now. I just wanted to think about things – that's all . . .'

'And he's sent you what – thirty-odd messages?'

'Yeah.'

'So call him, apologize for being crap and meet him somewhere, for God's sake.'

'But what if—?'

'That's it – I'm going. You're doing my head in now . . .'

'I'm sorry, Nat . . .' Just what I needed. My best friend getting pissed off with me too.

'Look – you haven't got time for this shit. We've all got GCSEs coming up. The last thing—'

'I don't know what to say,' I admitted, tears suddenly appearing.

'Don't cry, honey . . .'

'But Nat – he's going to hate me now.'

'Right, sod this. Get your little ass over here,' she demanded.

I thought about having to make up a reason to go out for my parents. 'I dunno if—'

'Rani – we're going to *revise* together, not have a sex-and-drugs-and-naughty-things party . . .'

'Let me ask – I'll call you back.'

Nat didn't reply straight away.

'*Nat?* You still there . . . ?'

'Tell you what,' she replied. 'Leave it for a couple of hours. Come round about five.'

'But you said to—'

'I've got a plan, Stan,' she said.

'Nat?'

But the line was dead.

I went downstairs about an hour later, after trying to concentrate on maths homework without success. My dad was in the living room, snoozing, and my mum was out in the jungle-like conservatory, watering her zillion and one plants. She heard me approach and turned to me.

'What do you want?' she asked in Punjabi.

'What makes you think that I want anything?' I said, pretending to be offended.

'Rani – you have on that face. Every time you want something you look like that.'

'I'm sorry for being alive,' I replied flippantly.

'Shut up! You never talk like that . . .' she told me.

'I just wanted to go over to my friend's to revise for my exams,' I said, waiting for her to say no.

'*Rebise?*' said my dad from behind us. He'd obviously woken up. And still not learned how to pronounce 'v's correctly, something lots of older Punjabis couldn't do.

'I want to go and revise at my friend's house,' I repeated.

'When?' he asked me, totally ignoring my mum's part in the conversation.

'Five o'clock,' I said. 'I'll be back by nine—'

'*Nine?*' he replied, going off the idea.

'Dad – it's only four hours . . . and Gurdip can pick me up later.'

The mention of my brother sealed the deal and my dad told me I could go, as long as I didn't turn off my mobile and only if I was really going to 'rebise' and not mess about.

'Dad, I've got my GCSEs in under five months. I want to do well . . .' So I can get out of here, I thought to myself.

'OK – *beteh* – you going,' he replied, in English this time. 'Ju calling Gurdip at the half-eight, telling him where to picking you up.'

'Thanks, Dad,' I said, before going back upstairs to ring Natalie.

# NATALIE & SUKH

Natalie stood outside Sukh's parents' house, wondering how much money it would take to buy such a big place. It was a mock–Tudor mansion with a double garage and long driveway. The iron gates at the front had a Sikh symbol as part of the overall design and the word BAINS. Very tasteful. She rang the bell again and then turned to admire the pebble driveway, sectioned off in three colours, white, brick-red and green. The borders were immaculate, with purple and green shrubs. Not a weed in sight. No one answered the door but from somewhere she could hear the beat of an R & B tune. She rang once again, wondering where everybody was and whether Sukh would get into trouble because a white girl was calling for him. It had been known to happen. In fact she had never even been round to her boyfriend Dev's house. Didn't know what it looked like or what his parents were like. She smiled as she remembered Dev telling her that it was an 'Indian' thing. She rang one more time.

Finally, deciding that no one was going to come to the door, Natalie walked round the side of the garages to a smaller gateway, through which she could see a landscaped garden. She debated whether or not she should try the gate, walk down the side of the house and try to get someone's attention. *Someone* was definitely in because they were playing a crappy tune by some generic R & B artist. By the time she had finished debating with herself, all of thirty seconds later, she was already standing underneath a veranda-style balcony at the back of the house, framed at the sides by ivy-covered trellises, the leaves a deep shade of green. Above her, the window furthest to her left was open, the source of the music. She called out to Sukh but got no reply.

Turning to face the garden, she saw a patio area made up of white pebbles and walked over to pick up a handful. From beneath the window she gently threw a pebble up. It hit the wall to the side, not really having the desired effect. She tried again, this time hitting the window with a slight tap. The third pebble flew in through the opening and announced her presence. *Someone* was in. *Someone* shouted a few very naughty words . . .

Sukh stuck his head out of the window, after turning his CD off, ready to shout at the idiot throwing pebbles, or to call the police if it was a burglar. As if he didn't have enough to deal with, he thought to himself. Down below him he saw Natalie and once the initial shock was gone, his stomach turned over.

Rani. It had to be about Rani . . .

'*Natalie!* What the fuck . . . ?'

'But, soft!' she began, a big smile cracking across her face, 'what light through yonder window breaks? It is the east and Sukhy boy, my son!'

'NAT! What—?'

'Sukhio! O Sukhio! Wherefore art thou Sukhio? Deny thy father and . . .'

Sukh groaned and considered finding the pebble that Nat had chucked through the window so that he could fling it at her stupid head. He couldn't see where it had landed. Instead he turned to Natalie again. 'What do you want, Natalie?'

Nat grinned up at him. 'So much for bloody romance!' she said. 'I'm here to see *you*. You lettin' me in or what?'

'What do you wanna see me about?'

'Doh! Whaddya think, sexy boy?'

Sukh groaned again and told her to go around to the front of the house. 'I'll be down in a minute.'

Natalie waited, as patiently as someone with her itchy feet could manage, for Sukh to open the door to her. When he eventually did she let him have another sickeningly sweet smile and asked him what had taken him so long.

'Nothing,' replied Sukh sullenly.

'Putting your trousers back on?' asked Nat, annoyingly.

'Look . . . what is it that you want, man?'

'Our mutual love is coming round to mine at five and I want you to be there,' said Natalie seriously.

'Why?' asked Sukh, trying to sound cool but spitting out his reply just a bit too quickly.

'Why do you think . . . ?'

Sukh looked away as he spoke, still trying to seem cool. 'She wants to see me she should reply to my messages an' that . . .'

'She feels stupid,' replied Natalie, unmoved by Sukh's attempted nonchalance, 'and, to be fair, she should.'

'What if I don't wanna see her?' asked Sukh.

'What if I just bang both your heads together?' said Natalie, meaning it.

'What if you just mind your own—?'

'Look – I don't have to be here,' Natalie reminded him. 'You want to carry on sitting around in your boxer shorts, listening to shite music and sending fifty messages an hour, that's your prerogative. *Me*, I'm just trying to help – so if you're gonna be all *wankyboy* about it . . .'

Sukh looked at her and then smiled for the first time in a week. 'I'm sorry,' he told her. 'I really *do* want to see her.'

'Thought as much,' said Natalie, taking his hand. 'Are you OK?'

Sukh took his hand away, regretting it instantly, and then looked to the floor. 'Yeah . . . No – I'm just . . .' He didn't really know what he was, apart from being just

a little excited at the thought of seeing Rani. Excited
and nervous too.

Natalie smiled warmly at him.

'Come in for bit,' he said. 'I need to have a shower.'

'Are you sure? Wouldn't wanna get into trouble with
Mummy and Daddy Bains.'

'Stop being such a dickhead, Nat, and wait in the
lounge,' he replied.

'Only thinking of your needs, Sukhy, my boy . . .'

'Shut up, Nat.'

Sukh showed Natalie into the living room, told her
not to break anything and to get herself a drink if she
wanted one, before heading up for a shower. Nat
thanked him, sat down on a deep, aubergine-coloured
leather sofa and waited.

SIX MONTHS LATER

 **RANI**

'What the hell is this?'
Sukh leaned across the bed and picked up the CD cover. He lay back and looked at it as I pushed up against his side, stroking the fine hairs on his chest.

'The Wailers,' he told me, like I was supposed to know who they were.

'Oh . . . *them*,' I said, pinching him on the hip.

'Oww!'

'Shut up, you fool . . .'

I pushed closer to him, trying to hold in my belly as I did so. It felt wrong, like I was due on, which I was in just under a week. But it was more tender than usual, probably because I had spent the entire weekend eating spicy food at the wedding of one of my cousins. Hence fat-belly girl. I wondered if Sukh had noticed and was being cute by not mentioning it, or whether he just didn't realize that I was fatter than I had been before I went away to Southall for the wedding.

'Says here that it's Bob Marley – you must have heard of him,' said Sukh, yawning.

181

'Yeah — everyone's heard of him but this doesn't sound anything like—'

'It's from the nineteen sixties.'

'What's this one?'

'*Stir It Up*,' he replied, showing me the cover.

'It sounds old . . . How come Parvy has all this stuff in her collection?' I asked.

'She likes to be eclectic,' he replied, running the tip of a finger along my shoulder and around and down to my breast.

'Thought we had to go in a bit,' I said, closing my eyes.

'We do,' he whispered, before finding my lips with his . . .

We got out of bed about an hour later. In the shower I stood thinking about the feud as the hot water blasted my face, and about how Sukh and I had left it all unsaid after getting back together. It was as though we had made a subconscious agreement to leave it alone and not talk about it. Ignore it. Not that I didn't think about it now and then. I'm sure that Sukh did too, but it really wasn't part of our lives — not the feud anyway. Avoiding my family had become second nature for us, but we'd have done that without a feud — it was what loads of Asian teenagers had to do. We weren't any different. There was just more at stake if my family, in particular, ever found out.

Not that Sukh's parents knew about *me* either. Parvy

had said that it wasn't worth telling them until we had decided that things were getting serious for us – like marriage-serious. Sukh had told me on more than one occasion that he didn't think his family would mind. That his parents were easy-going about girls and relationships. But even with their liberal outlook, I was still likely to come as a shock for them – just like I had for Parvy. And it was a shock that could wait for now. We had our GCSE results to come and things were stressful enough.

The good thing about having finished school was that I could spend a lot more time with Sukh. We'd been like strangers in the final run-up to exams, both of us determined to do as well as we could so that we'd get into Queen Elizabeth, the sixth-form college near the university, ten minutes' walk from Parvy's flat. I also spent more time, if that was possible, with Natalie, who was still seeing Dev. Nat was scared that she hadn't done well at her weaker subjects like maths and science, especially as she had her career mapped out, aiming for RADA or an equivalent drama college. She called it her three-step programme to a Bafta.

I smiled to myself as I thought about it and then turned the shower off. I could hear Sukh moving around in the flat, and I got dressed and joined him in the living room.

'You smell great,' he said, sniffing my hair.

'You sayin' I didn't smell great before?' I joked.

'Well – I didn't want to say . . .'

I punched him and then, more seriously, I asked him if he thought I was fat.

'Don't be silly, beautiful,' he replied, grinning. 'You're perfect.'

'You might just be saying that,' I told him. 'You could be one of them pervs who likes to fatten up their girl-friends . . .'

Sukh shook his head. 'You're a funny bird, some-times,' he said.

'So you don't think that I'm fat?'

'Rani – you're not fat. You're perfect.'

I couldn't let it go though. 'I've put on weight over the weekend,' I complained.

'Not that I can see,' he said, picking up his jacket from the sofa.

'I feel like I have.'

'And what we've just been doing has worked it all off,' he grinned.

'I'm serious . . .'

'So am I, Rani. You look fantastic, in and out of your clothes.'

'But . . .'

'Come here,' he said, hugging me and kissing my forehead.

'You would tell me, wouldn't you – if you thought that I was turning into a heifer?'

Sukh squeezed me tight and told me that he loved me. I smiled at that and then let my neuroses go.

'Come on – I've got to meet the football team for

practice at six,' he said.

'Oh shit – I need to get home . . .' I replied, wondering which excuse I was going to use on my dad this time.

When I got in my dad was far too angry about something else to even care where I had come from. He was pacing the living room, a tumbler of whisky and Coke in his hands, swearing at someone or something in Punjabi. I looked at my mum who gave me a don't-ask look and then scurried off into the kitchen. Divy was sitting in an armchair, wearing a long black leather coat that made him look like some sort of gangster. I smiled at him but he was wearing a scowl to go with his coat and didn't smile back or ask me how I was.

My dad turned to him and spoke in Punjabi. 'How long have they had the shop?' he asked.

'I don't know but they're opening next week. Opposite us. Same lines, same everything. And menswear too.'

My dad swore. He took a long drink of whisky and then swore some more.

'Let me deal with them,' said Divy. 'You've retired.'

'No,' replied my dad sternly. 'This is not something you can deal with using your fists, Divinder.'

'What's happening, Dad?' I asked, alerted to the mention of fists.

'Nothing, *beteh*. You go and make the dinner with your mother. This is for us men to sort out.'

'With your fists? It must be serious,' I replied.

'Why don't you listen when you're told to do something?' snapped Divy in English.

'Was I talking to you?' I asked, angry at his tone of voice.

'This is about the business which, once you're married off to some other family, ain't gonna be your concern.'

'You stupid—'

'*BETEH!*' shouted my dad. 'Leaving it, please.'

I glared at my brother and then at my dad.

'Mind your own business, Rani,' said Divy, before returning to the conversation and pretending that I wasn't in the room. 'They have to pay,' he said to my dad in Punjabi.

'No! Let the bastards open their shop. We will open a bigger one, with cheaper stock—'

'But these fucking Bains . . .'

My heart started pounding in my chest. 'Who are the Bains?' I asked, but the look that I got from both of them sent me out to the kitchen to help my mum. Behind me the door slammed shut, shaking the frame.

'Mum, what's this about someone called Bains?' I asked, my heart still racing.

'Just some business enemies,' said my mum, not looking at me; hiding something. Only I knew what it was.

'Who?'

'Nothing for you to worry about, *beteh*. This is an old problem . . .'

'How old?'

'Long, long time, Rani. Now get your hands washed – we need to start the dinner—'

'Is it like a feud or something?' I asked, taking a risk by leading her.

'*Rani!* Do not answer back to me.'

'God! I was only asking . . .'

My mum relented a bit when she saw the hurt on my face. I thought about Nat in that split second. I wondered whether I should be the one applying to RADA.

'The Bains are very bad people – our families do not like each other . . .' she told me, as if that was enough to explain everything.

'Why?' I asked, pushing it further.

'Nothing for you to know about – your father will kill me if he knows I have told you.'

'Oh don't be such a drama queen!' I said to her, but something in her eyes made me realize that she believed her own words. She whispered her reply, keeping one eye on the kitchen door, scared that my dad might walk in.

'It is a very old feud – something from the Punjab. They killed someone in our family and they have tried to take our business away here in England—'

'*Killed?*' I pretended to be shocked.

'It is nothing for you to know, *beteh*,' repeated my mum.

'But—'

'Now they are opening a shop opposite ours, in The Shires, and your brother is unhappy about it. They are just trying to be as good as us.'

I waited, hoping that now she was talking, she would tell me some more. She did.

'We opened a factory – the first one, and they copied us. We opened some shops and they did the same. We moved here to Oadby and bought a lovely big house and they did that too. It's as though they are trying to be better than us at everything.'

'Maybe they're not doing it to upset us,' I said. 'Maybe they are just doing the same as us – trying to be successful.'

'*No!* They are not like us. We are bigger than them.' She looked as if she wanted to spit out their name. As if it was a nasty taste in her mouth.

'How do you know what they are like if you don't even speak to—?'

'Enough! Are you taking their side against your own family?'

My heart somersaulted and I felt sick, a strange metallic taste making its way up from my food pipe into my throat. I swallowed and held it back but I was feeling nauseous.

'Now go and wash your hands. And never tell your father that I have told you anything,' she whispered.

I nodded, trying not to let her see that I was going to be sick. I turned and hurried out of the kitchen, running up the stairs and into my bedroom. I could hear shouting coming from the living room. I ran into my bathroom and threw up, my head spinning, and the metallic taste burning my throat. I threw up about four times and then I cleaned myself up, wondering whether I should call Sukh and tell him what was happening.

 **RANI**

Sukh rang me back after he'd heard the message I had left him. He was dismissive of it all – joking about it.

'It's serious, Sukh. What if they find out about us?'

It was the first time I had seriously considered what would happen if we were discovered since hearing all about the feud. Before I knew our family histories the idea that we would be seen by my brothers or my dad had already been scary. But now it was enough to make me feel sick to my stomach. It had *made* me sick to my stomach.

'They won't – and anyway this shop thing isn't anything to do with my dad. I'd know if we were going to open a new outlet.'

'It has to be . . . my brother mentioned your family . . .'

'It might be one of my uncles. The whole family's into the rag trade.'

I hadn't even considered that it might not be Sukh's dad. 'Oh,' I said quietly.

'Look – what happened is way in the past. We've

already decided that it's not going to affect us – not yet anyway. Why worry about it when it ain't gonna happen, honey?'

'But it might . . .'

'Rani—'

'No, Sukh,' I replied, raising my voice. 'You don't know my dad or Divy—'

'*Divy?*'

'Yeah – my oldest brother,' I told him.

'Does he drive a black Audi?' asked Sukh.

'Yeah . . . why?' For some reason I began to feel a little sick again.

'I saw him down the park when we had a game once. Has he got a ponytail and a long black leather coat . . . ?'

'Yeah.'

'*That's* your brother?'

'Sukh – you're scaring me now . . .' I said, worried that there was something else going on that I didn't know about.

'It's nothing – honest. I've just seen him around,' he replied, trying to reassure me.

Something in his voice told me that he was hiding something. I was going to push it but then I let it go. My stomach felt rough again and I tasted that strange metallic tang again. 'I'll call you tomorrow,' I told him abruptly.

'Rani? You OK?'

'Yeah – I'm just feeling a bit queasy. It's all that fried

food at the wedding – I'll be fine.'

'Look, if there's anything wrong—' he began, before I cut him off.

'Gotta go, beautiful boy,' I said bravely, hoping that he would believe I was in a good mood and not about to throw my guts up again.

'OK. Love you . . .'

'Me too . . .'

I rang off, chucked the phone on my bed and ran to the bathroom.

Later that evening I tried to get my mum to tell me more but she refused to budge. In the end I sat in the living room with my dad, watching television and hoping that he would start ranting about what was going on. He'd had a few drinks already and was holding another one as I sat there. I watched him out of the corner of my eye, his face glum and his bottom lip protruding like a sad child.

'You OK, Dad?' I asked.

He looked at me and I could see that he was tearful. '*Beteh*, you do not know what you mean to me,' he said.

'I do, Dad,' I replied, suddenly feeling all emotional.

'*Nah, beteh* – it is not for your understanding . . .' He looked at his drink, swallowed some and then began to speak in Punjabi. 'So much happened to us before you came along. We had to deal with so much—'

'Dad . . .'

'You know – once, a long time ago, I lost two of my friends. Together. At the same time . . .'

'Who?'

He drank some more and looked away at a picture of Guru Nanak, which hung on the wall above the fireplace. 'The Lord took from me my best friend and someone else . . .' he slurred.

I wanted him to carry on, to finally tell me in his own words about the sister he had lost, the aunt that I had never been told about. But he just started to cry and I couldn't handle it. Dads were strong and jolly and full of fun. They didn't sit around drowning their sorrows in whisky and telling sad tales, at least not in my perfect world. It got too hard for me to sit there, so I stood up, trying not to cry. My dad got up too and gave me a hug that nearly crushed the wind out of me. I could smell the whisky on his breath.

'You are my only daughter,' he said, 'my only . . .'

And then suddenly he exploded with rage, letting go of me and throwing his glass at the wall. 'Let them try and take you away! Let them!'

My heart did yet another somersault. For a split second, my world with Sukh crashed before my eyes and I thought, *believed*, that he knew about us . . .

'Daddy-ji, I—'

'Kulwant . . .' he said in a whisper, slumping into the sofa and beginning to cry.

I looked at him, tears flowing down my cheeks and then looked away. I wanted to tell him right there and then. I felt guilty and scared and as though I had let him down . . . but the story that Parvy had told me was right there at the forefront of my thoughts and part of me got angry. I wanted to ask him about it; to ask why they had destroyed those two young people over love. Over something so meaningful and natural . . .

Sukh's face entered my mind then and I left the room, walking slowly up to my bedroom, listening to my dad sobbing, as he remembered a time when he had been best friends with Sukh's dad, and the two of them had bragged about seeing snakes and hunting for witches . . .

 **RANI**

The following morning Nat opened the door to her mum's house in her underwear and smiled. 'Hey, sexy girl,' she said, looking out into the road.

'Put some clothes on, you tart,' I told her, embarrassed for her, and secretly envious of her body.

'No one can see me,' she replied. 'Anyway – it's no worse than opening the door in a bikini.'

'Nat – it's way different.' God, I wish I had that stomach, I thought as I stood there.

She ushered me in and closed the door before walking me into the lounge. 'Sit down – I'll just go and get dressed,' she told me, with a smile.

She returned five minutes later in a pair of beige combats, white trainers and a tight white T-shirt with a red love heart on it. Sitting down on the sofa beside me, she tucked her feet under her and asked me what was wrong. I started by telling her what was going on with my family – the way my brother had talked about the Bainses and then the episode with my dad, right down to the tears and everything. When I'd finished, Nat sat for a while and said nothing, which was amazing for her.

'There's more too,' I said, after a while.

'*More?* I'm gonna have to write this all down, babe.'

'I'm fat,' I said, looking away.

'Rani . . .'

'I've put weight on. I asked Sukh about it but he just told me I was beautiful and he always does that.'

Nat shook her head and moved closer. 'You're not fat, Rani.'

'I am,' I insisted. 'I went away for that wedding and ate too much and now I'm bloater-girl and my belly's swollen and my tits are sore and—'

'Easy, easy, Rani. Take a breath before you turn blue, babe.'

'And my stomach's been playing up, although that's probably due to the fact that I've been given food poisoning by my silly aunt who didn't cook the food properly . . .' I continued, after taking a breath as instructed.

'Are you due on?' asked Nat, shifting so that she was facing me.

'Yeah – in a couple of days . . .'

'And you've been taking precautions?' she said seriously.

I looked at her, blinked and then realized what she was on about. 'I'm not pregnant,' I told her, as my mind filled with images of the toilet bowl in my bathroom. I'd been seeing a lot of it since the weekend.

'Rani – condoms can split—'

'Well, that's not happened to us. I'm not pregnant!' I protested.

Nat took my hand and smiled. 'You're probably just a bit hormonal – it's the same every month. You get all tearful over silly little things and you tell me you're fat.'

'No I don't,' I protested, as tears welled in my eyes and I looked down at the water-retaining, blubber-covered excuse for a body that I had been born with.

'*See?* You're just rubbish sometimes,' said Nat, proving her point.

'I know – I can't help it,' I admitted.

'No worries, babe – it's one of the reasons I love you so much.'

She leaned across and planted a big kiss on my lips. 'Now, we going to sit around here feeling sorry for ourselves or are we going to go into town, drink alcohol and look at really expensive clothes that we can't afford?' she said, pinching my cheek.

'Can't we just hang out for a bit?' I asked, not ready to face the world just at that point.

'Yeah, all right – we can pop into town later. Do you want a drink?'

I told her that I wanted a cup of tea, and as she was making it I sent Sukh a text asking him what he was up to.

 **SUKH**

Sukh pressed the SEND button on his phone and then put it back into his jacket pocket. He put the jacket in his sports holdall and placed it in the boot of his cousin Ranjit's Vectra, which was parked down by the side of Victoria Park on an overcast but humid Saturday morning. Ranjit was sitting in the driver's seat, door open, with bhangra, hip-hop style, pounding the bass bin.

'What time we kicking off?'

Sukh looked round and saw his mate Jaspal, standing beside him in his football kit, complete with his boots.

'Not for half an hour – the other team ain't even here yet, Jas.'

'Oh, right. Thought it was about now.'

Sukh smiled. 'You wanna take those boots off, Jas. You'll kill the studs walking about on the pavement – scuff 'em down.'

Jas looked down his long, spindly legs at his Adidas Predators and then back at Sukh. 'We may as well go on the grass and have a warm-up,' he replied.

Sukh went to the boot and got out one of the three footballs he could see. He tossed it to Jas, who tried to control it on his chest but the ball bounced off at an awkward angle and rolled into Victoria Park Road. Jas swore and clattered after it, before returning to Sukh.

'Come on,' he said, giving the ball a whack so that it shot high into the air and landed with a soft thud on the grass.

Sukh followed Jas onto the grass by the side of the football pitch. Cars were parked all along the road and other Asian lads sat listening to bhangra, got changed or stood around smoking and drinking from cans of Coke and Fanta. Ahead of Sukh, the park stretched out into the distance, across other football pitches, a cricket match, down towards the university, with its tall buildings, and way over to De Montfort Hall to the right. To the left of the uni stood QE sixth-form college, where Sukh was hoping to go after the summer: A levels in Politics, Psychology and Economics. He thought for a moment about his GCSEs and nearly started worrying about his results. But his thoughts were cut short by the football, which whacked him on his left thigh, leaving a stinging sensation.

'You knob!' he shouted at Jaspal, who just stood and giggled at him like a pre-teen schoolgirl.

They spent about twenty minutes knocking the ball around between them, juggling it from foot to foot and trying to perform the tricks they'd seen real footballers do. As they did so, more and more young men from both teams arrived by the side of the pitch, and eventually the players got themselves ready for action. It was a Saturday League game for under-eighteens and Ranjit had picked the team: Sukh was starting the game this time and he was looking forward to it. Three other games were being played and, one by one, they all kicked off as the sun broke through the gloom and the temperature began to rise.

Sukh played well for the first half, setting up four clear chances, one of which gave his team a deserved half-time lead, but then Ranjit, eager to give as many players a run-out as he could before the round of summer tournaments kicked in, took him off. Sukh didn't complain. He was tired and thirsty, and he joined the other substitutes and supporters on the touchline, where he stood drinking from a carton of warm orange juice, watching the match unfold. The second half dragged a bit, with only one more goal scored by Sukh's replacement, an older lad called Manny. It ended two–nil, and slowly both sets of players began to trudge off towards their cars.

Sukh was waiting for Ranjit to finish taking down the goal posts when he saw Tej and Manj walking over from the direction of the pub on London Road. Both of them looked half cut already and Sukh hoped they were just coming over to say hello before going on their way. Some hope. Manj, holding a bottle of lager, grabbed Sukh around the shoulders with his free arm.

'SUKHY!' he shouted, pulling him in close. 'What you sayin', man?'

'All right, Coz,' replied Sukh, trying to get away.

'*Aw kiddah?*' added Tej, throwing a fake punch at Sukh's stomach.

'I'm all right, Tej. Can't you say hello in English?'

Tej grinned and drank from his bottle. 'English-Pinglish! Fuck it!' he shouted, before taking another swig.

'We's goin' over to another game, Sukhy. The senior side are playin' the enemy,' added Manj.

'Bloody Sandhu FC,' said Tej, grinning again.

Sukh thought about Rani. Part of him wanted to tell his cousins that he was going home, that he had things to do, people to see. But he also wanted to go on over to the other game and see what happened. To watch the feud play itself out, looking at it through his new-found knowledge. He turned to his cousins. 'Cool – I'll come over, but I ain't getting into no shit because of you two,' he told them.

'Trouble? *Us?*' laughed Manj.

'Trouble–schmubble,' added Tej.

Jaspal and a few of the other lads were still hanging around and they joined Sukh and his cousins for the walk over to the senior game. Sukh trailed behind the rest with Ranjit, wondering why he was going along, yet unable to stop himself. As they approached the pitch, Sukh realized that there were at least sixty people gathered round, split equally on either touchline. He

201

found a space on his own side and glanced across the pitch to the other team's supporters. Divy Sandhu was standing with a group of three other men, wearing his leather coat, his hair tied back in a ponytail, talking into a mobile. The men with him were laughing and gesturing across the pitch, occasionally shouting out insults in Punjabi. Tej, Manj and a few of the others threw back their own insults. None of them seemed particularly interested in the game itself, which was scrappy. As Sukh watched, Divy pocketed his mobile and turned to one of his crew, gesturing across the pitch as he spoke. The man he spoke to nodded and said something to the other two, and the three of them began to walk around the pitch towards the opposing fans. Sukh looked at Tej for a reaction, but Tej hadn't noticed – he was busy calling the referee names. Sukh saw Divy say something to another couple of lads and then join them, as they too headed for where Sukh was standing.

He turned to Manj. 'Yo – you better check out what's coming,' he told him.

'Wha'?'

Sukh nodded towards the group of Sandhu men walking around the pitch, their faces set in stony masks.

Manj saw them and poked Tej on the back. 'Tej – better get some lads together. We got some trouble . . .'

Tej realized what was happening straight away and called out some names. A few of Sukh's cousins and second cousins gathered together, one or two of them emptying their bottles of lager onto the grass and holding them at their sides. Tej put a hand into his jacket and pulled out a cosh. His eyes were blazing and he pushed Sukh out of the way, making his way towards the fast-approaching Sandhus.

Sukh looked at Ranjit, who stood with his shoulders squared, ready to fight. 'Ranjit – what the fuck's going on?' he asked, beginning to get worried.

'Somethin' happened down the pub last night – between Tej and them wankers.' He nodded towards Rani's brother.

'*What?*' repeated Sukh.

'Tej's old man is opening up near them Sandhus – in The Shires – and they ain't having it. That Divy's been threatening us all over town, man.'

Sukh realized that he already knew about it. Rani had told him. Only it was Sukh's uncle and not his father who had offended the Sandhus. He shook his head and decided that he would stay out of it. He took a few steps away, only for Ranjit to grab him by the arm.

'Where you goin', Sukh?'

'I ain't part of this, Ranj. Ain't my business . . .'

Ranjit spat out the gum he had been chewing. 'This is *our* business, Sukh. *Bains* business.' The look in his eyes challenged Sukh to show where his loyalties lay.

Sukh shrugged and shook his head. 'I don't wanna fight them. What they ever done to me?' he said.

Before Ranjit could reply a bottle hurtled through the air and caught him on the side of his head, knocking him to the ground. Sukh span round, just in time to catch a bottle in the face. He hit the ground holding his cheek, which felt hot and wet. He looked at his hand and saw the blood. Gazing up he saw a full-scale riot taking place, with thirty or so men involved. He stood up gingerly and felt a shove in the back. He stumbled but stayed upright, turned and saw Manj and Divy going at it, with Divy gaining the upper hand. Manj dropped to his knees after getting a kick in the balls, coughing and retching at the same time. Divy pulled a bottle from his coat and pulled back his arm—

Sukh caught him on the temple, from the side, with a strong right, following it with a short left jab to the back of his head. Divy staggered, dropped the bottle and went down from a stomach punch that flew in from Steve, one of the footballers.

Divy looked up at Sukh, grinning, as police sirens wailed and people ran for cover. 'You're dead,' he told Sukh.

'I ain't got nothing against you . . .' replied Sukh, his hand pressed against the gash in his face.

'You fucking dog! You throw sly punches and then tell me you don't mean no harm . . .' Divy sucked in air.

'I was trying to stop you. You could have killed Manj . . .'

Divy stood up as policemen ran to the scene.

'I ain't got nothing against you, Divy,' repeated Sukh, as a policeman grabbed him from behind.

'You're a fucking Bains,' spat Divy. 'That's enough . . .'

Sukh pictured Rani's face, heard her words and shook his head. 'We're closer than you think,' he told Divy, who lunged for him, only to be dragged back by two policemen.

'You an' me ain't nothing but enemies, Bains – remember that,' added Divy as he was dragged away.

Sukh was taken to the Royal Infirmary and stitched up. The gash could have been worse, but he was still going to have to explain what happened to his parents. And, more importantly, to Rani. The police questioned him but didn't arrest him. They realized that he had been a victim and urged him to tell them who had bottled him. Sukh told them that he hadn't seen who it was. Asked about Divy, he shook his head. He hadn't seen Divy until they had started arguing. The argument had been over nothing, just a testosterone-fuelled slanging match. The policeman interviewing Sukh at the hospital had been suspicious, but in the end, five hours after the fight, the doctors allowed him to go home, where he found his parents waiting for him. He deflected their questions too, letting his dad blame Sukh's cousins, and told them that he had to go to bed: doctor's orders.

In his room he sat and looked at his mobile, the

lights flashing that he had three missed calls and four text messages, all but one from Rani. He wondered what he was going to tell her before deciding that he'd tell the truth. He didn't want to lie to her, or hide stuff from her. He couldn't. He picked up a glass of water and swallowed two painkillers, lay back in his bed and closed his eyes, his cheek tingling and itchy underneath the dressing and his mind showing the same three-second clip over and over. Divy, spitting words of hatred, and then a flash of Rani's smile . . .

 **RANI**

The first thing I did the next morning was check my mobile, hoping that Sukh had sent me a message. The last one had been sent the previous afternoon, letting me know that he was playing football. I hadn't heard anything from him since, and I was feeling a bit pissed off. I'd tried to contact him several times but he'd ignored me. Or at least that was how it had felt the previous evening, when I had called Nat and moaned about it. I had these silly thoughts going round in my head – like maybe I had upset him or he'd gone off me for being fat. Nat had told me off for being so insecure, and asked me to consider the possibility that Sukh might have gone out with his friends, got pissed and gone home to sleep it off. It was an explanation that was probably closer to the truth than the one that had kept me awake, worrying about why he hadn't called me.

Now, I lay on my back, staring up at the ceiling, willing the mobile to ring or at least flash a message at me. Twenty minutes after I had opened my eyes it had done neither. I got out of bed, wondering where Sukh

207

had got to, feeling a little queasy. My stomach was tight and hard, the back of my throat dry. I went to the bathroom and cleaned my teeth, realizing that I needed a towel. I put on a dressing gown and went out into the hallway. Voices, loud and male, greeted me. I could make out my dad and Divy and Gurdip, but there were others too. At least two more voices, raised and argumentative. I grabbed a towel from the airing cupboard and went back into my room, looking at my clock. It was ten on a Sunday morning and my family were arguing downstairs. I picked up my phone. No message. Then I had an awful thought . . . Sukh hadn't called and my family were downstairs, early on a Sunday . . .

Five minutes later, with my hair hastily tied up and wearing jeans and a T-shirt, I was standing in the hallway, listening to the argument. I edged towards the door to the front living room and pushed it open a little more. The argument seemed to be about a fight of some sort, the voices raging in Punjabi. I pushed the door open fully and walked in. Alongside Divy, Gurdip and my dad were two of my uncles, Sohan and Kewal, and a cousin, all sitting around, not touching the tea and samosas in front of them.

'GET OUT!'

I jumped, glaring at Divy.

My dad looked at me. 'Don't shout at my daughter,' he said to Divy quietly, before turning to me.

'*Beteh*, please leave us alone. Go and help your mother . . .'

I was about to say something, but quickly realized that it would have been a bad move. Instead I stood for a moment and gawped at the bruises on Divy's face, praying that he hadn't got them fighting Sukh's family, but knowing that my prayer was in vain. Why else would my uncles be round so early on a Sunday morning instead of being down at the *gurudwara*, bragging about how much money they had given to the building fund.

'Are you *deaf*?' spat Divy, getting up and walking towards me, his clothes crumpled and creased, as though he had slept in them.

'What happened to your—?' I began, as he pushed me out of the room and shut the door.

I stood in the hallway, fuming, until my mother called me into the kitchen. I called Divy a few names, only for my mum to defend the macho idiot.

'He is your brother, Rani,' she told me in Punjabi, as she fried more samosas that weren't going to be touched.

'What you frying them for?' I replied in English. 'They haven't touched the last lot.'

My mum ignored me and went about her business. I opened the fridge and poured myself some water.

'Eat something,' said my mum, as I emptied my glass.

'I'm not hungry,' I said. 'At least not for samosas.

They don't exactly make a healthy breakfast . . .'

'Up to you,' replied my mum, dismissing me with her tone of voice.

'What's going on in there?' I asked her in Punjabi, gesturing to the hallway and beyond.

'Nothing . . .'

'And I'm supposed to believe that?' I said.

'Family business,' replied my mum, draining the samosas before pouring more tea into a steel kettle.

'What business are we in nowadays – one that leaves Divy with bruises all over his face?'

'Leave it, Rani. It's for the men to sort out . . .'

I sighed. 'This is about that feud, isn't it? With the Bainses?'

My mum looked at me, then looked away before she replied. 'There was a fight yesterday – at a football match . . .'

I don't know what my face looked like as I leaned against a worktop, but my mum picked up on it straight away. My stomach was doing its daily ritual of twisting and turning and forcing bile up into my throat.

'What's the matter, *beteh*?' she asked, a concerned look on her face.

'Nothing,' I lied.

'*Rani?*'

'I just feel a bit sick – that's all. It's the smell from the frying—'

'If you will eat English food all the time, what do you expect?'

This time it was my turn to look anywhere but at my mum. I walked over to the kitchen table and sat down, forcing back bile. My head was swimming with thoughts. Sukh hadn't contacted me – which meant he must be in trouble or something. My brother was walking around in the same clothes he'd been wearing the day before, with a plum-sized knot next to his eye, and my family were at what looked like a war council, with me and my mum banished to the kitchen. Sukh, whose last text had said he was playing football. Sukh, who had reacted in a funny way when he found out that Divy was my brother . . .

Right on cue, Divy walked into the kitchen with my dad, his face set in a frown. Immediately my mum began to fuss over him, in a way she never did with me.

'*Beteh*, let me look at your face . . .' she said, as my dad told her to stop fussing.

'If he will get into fights then he will get hurt,' my dad told her in Punjabi.

'Who did you fight with?' asked my mum.

Divy pushed her hands away, found a mug and poured himself some spiced tea. 'No one, Mum – it's nothing,' he lied.

My dad looked at me, tried to smile and then turned to my mum. 'With Resham's boy,' he told her, his voice soft and calm.

I swallowed some more bile and tried not to let it show in my face. Not easy to do, believe me.

'*Resham*,' replied my mum, more as a statement than a question.

My dad's face clouded over, his eyes telling me that his thoughts were far away somewhere. My mum walked over to Divy, who had joined me at the table, his mouth open as he chewed his samosa. I tried not to look at him.

'Which one?' my mum asked Divy, who didn't say anything.

My dad replied for him. 'The youngest one . . . Sukhjit . . .' he said.

I nearly threw up on the spot, fighting to hold it back. I stood up, ready to make a run for the bathroom, but with my stomach under control again. I swallowed hard, realizing for myself that even though my father hadn't spoken to Sukh's dad for years, the Punjabi grapevine meant that both our families knew everything about each other.

'*Hai Rabbah* – will these Bains never leave us alone?' my mum whispered to God.

'When they learn their lesson,' spat Divy. 'That boy learned his yesterday—'

'And what if the police had arrested you?' replied my dad.

Arrested for what? I looked at my brother.

'He ain't dead – it was just a scratch . . .' he said, getting up from his chair.

I stood up at the same time, mumbled something about feeling sick and went up to my bathroom as

212

quickly as I could, reaching the bowl just in time, as the voices began to rise again downstairs and my brother and father rejoined the other men.

After I had cleaned myself up I sent Sukh another message. No greeting. No declarations of love. Just a simple text.

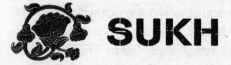 **SUKH**

Sukh felt his left cheek tingling and itching beneath the dressing. He wanted to touch it. To scratch it. Instead he opened and closed his jaw and instantly wished that he hadn't as tears flooded to his eyes. His left eye twitched slightly and then the pain calmed down a little. He was going to have to take another painkiller. He hadn't had a chance to call Rani either, but that would have to wait. He had some explaining to do.

He looked over at his dad, who was busy reading the paper, ignoring him. Making a point. Sukh tried to explain again. That it wasn't his fault. That he had been acting as a peacemaker. His dad looked at him over the top of his paper.

'You are an idiot,' he said, repeating the same words he had used all morning.

'Dad – I was *trying* to break it up . . .' protested Sukh, as loudly as he could manage.

His dad folded and rolled up the paper and gave Sukh his full attention. 'You are scarred for life, *beteh*,' he said, using the paper to gesture towards his son.

'Nah – it ain't *that* bad . . . it'll fade,' reassured Sukh.

'Why did you going in first place?'

'I didn't *go* anywhere, Dad – I was already there. It was after our game ended. I went over to see the seniors play with Ranjit and everyone—'

'*Tej and bloody Manjit? Drunks?* Some game you watching . . .'

Sukh touched the dressing lightly as his mum walked into the room with a cup of coffee for his dad. She shook her head at Sukh and sat down as his dad continued his lecture, switching to Punjabi.

'Time and time again I tell you to stay away from those two and you do your best to make sure that you get into as much trouble as possible. Well, their fathers are going to be here soon and we are going to get this sorted out—'

'Dad – it was—'

'No!' interrupted his dad, slapping the rolled-up paper against the coffee table, spilling the fresh cup that his wife had made him.

'*Fucking*— I try to hide this bloody mess from you . . . protect you . . . !' he shouted in broken English.

Sukh rarely heard his dad swear and knew that he was upset and angry. He looked at his mum, who seemed to be as angry as his dad.

'What you young 'uns know 'bout it, eh? Bastard playing games – that's what you all doing. This not a game, Sukhjit.'

'Look at your *face*, *beteh*,' added his mum, with a touch more warmth.

Sukh thought of Rani and agreed with his dad. Silently and for different reasons. But an agreement all the same.

'You begin fight all over again – when it should be putting in past where it belonging . . .'

Sukh felt himself getting angry as his cheek did its tingling thing and his left eye twitched some more. He listened as his dad went on, trying to calm himself and failing.

'It was Divy Sandhu!' he shouted, cutting his dad off midstream, not expecting the reaction that he got.

Resham Bains sat and stared out at nothing, his mouth slightly open, his eyes filling up. He looked at his son, blinked back tears and looked away again. When he eventually spoke it was in a whisper. 'Mohinder's son,' he said, not waiting for a reply.

Sukh thought about saying yes but caught himself. Did he really want his father to know that he had learned the real story of the feud from Parvy? He worked out that the answer was no. He had a strong feeling that his dad was going to tell him about it anyway. And he was right.

'Mohinder Sandhu was my childhood friend,' began Sukh's dad. 'My brother . . .'

He told Sukh most of the story, much the same one as Parvy had told, all the while stopping to apologize to Sukh for hiding the truth from him. 'I wanted you to grow up without all of this,' he reasoned.

When the story was told, Resham Bains looked at

his youngest son and then let a tear fall. Sukh swallowed hard. He'd never seen his dad react to anything with tears. It was a strange moment, like a new thread linking the two of them together, one that went beyond the normal father–son bonds. Sukh felt his wound and then opened his mouth and let words fall out, not thinking or caring about the consequences.

'I know his daughter. Rani.'

He expected a reaction but didn't get one. His dad shed a few more tears and continued talking, ignoring what Sukh had just said. Sukh looked to his mother, who frowned at him, rose from her seat and left the room. Sukh realized that she had taken in what he'd admitted – not that it was much. He turned to his dad.

'Why can't this feud stay buried in the past, where it belongs?' he asked.

'*Beteh* – I have asked myself the same question over and over. Both our families lost children. I lost two brothers that day, Billah and Mohinder. But your uncles and cousins continue to let the past cloud the future too.'

'But why continue the feud? Can't you just talk to Mohinder?'

His dad looked at him with resignation etched across his face. 'And say *what*, Sukhjit? That I am sorry that his father killed my brother?'

'But it means that the feud will just go on . . .' argued Sukh.

'It has been going for too long, *beteh*. Nothing can

bring our families together now.'

Sukh thought about Rani again. What if there was something . . . ? 'Dad – what if there *was* something that could do it – help to sort out the problems . . . ?'

His dad sighed. 'There is nothing, Sukhjit. *Nothing . . .* ' he replied, shaking his head.

Sukh was about to reply when his mobile bleeped a message at him. He picked it up and read the words on the tiny screen.

 **RANI**

'Does it hurt?'

Sukh shook his head and tried to smile. The effort made him wince and I could tell that he wasn't telling the truth. It had to hurt. It was horrible.

'I'm sorry,' I said.

'Sorry for *what*? Ain't your fault.'

'It was *my* brother . . .'

'Yeah – well you ain't your brother and anyway I didn't have to get involved.'

I leaned across Parvy's sofa and touched his other cheek softly. I thought he would pull away, tell me to stop. We'd met at the flat the morning after, and hadn't kissed each other or anything. There was something between us, like a kind of invisible wall holding us back. The wall was my brother. Or so I thought. But Sukh didn't flinch or move away so I felt secure enough to move across to him and kiss him where I had just touched him. He turned his head towards mine and kissed me back and then he said sorry.

'It's not your fault, either,' I told him.

'I didn't even see it coming. Just turned my head—'

219

'And it was Divy . . .'

'Dunno. He started the whole thing but I didn't see who—'

'No – it *was* Divy. I heard him tell my dad about it.'

'Whatever – it was stupid . . .'

I took my hand and touched his wounded cheek this time, stroking him gently. I had been sick again that morning and still felt nauseous. I wanted to tell him, to find out what he would say. What he would think about it. But then again, he was a boy and what would he know about it? My mind started wandering through a minefield of different thoughts – different reasons for my feeling sick all the time, not once letting me settle on what might well be the real reason. That I was pregnant. I shivered.

'What's up, babe?' asked Sukh, feeling me tremble.

'It's nothing – just been a bit sick, that's all.'

'Maybe you've got a bug coming on or something . . .'

Maybe I'm just not going to come on, I thought to myself.

'Yeah, maybe,' I replied, closing my eyes as I pulled up against him.

'So – what we gonna do?' he asked, stroking my hair.

'There's nothing we can do,' I said, feeling a little calmer. Not for long though.

'We could just tell them,' suggested Sukh.

I pulled away and looked at him. '*Tell them?*' I asked, astonished.

'Yeah . . . maybe get them all together and—'

'Sukh, have you gone *mad*?'

I couldn't believe what he was saying. There we were, together, when our families hated each other and fought all the time, with me possibly pregnant, and he was talking about telling them.

'Just think about it for a minute, Rani. I kind of let slip to my dad that we know each other—'

'*Sukh . . .*' I was shaking.

'He didn't even *hear* me—'

'You *told* him?'

'Rani – believe me – he had other things on his mind. He was going all misty-eyed and talking about your dad and how they used to be best friends.'

'Just like my dad . . .'

'Yeah – so why don't we just tell them and get them together. Maybe we can end this whole stupid mess—'

'*No!*'

Sukh looked at me, raising an eyebrow. 'Just like that? No?'

'Even if my dad did go along with it – which he won't because he's already threatened to throw me out into the street if he ever catches me going out with someone – but even if he does, Divy won't ever let it lie.'

'But surely if your dad comes round, then Divy can't say fuck all.'

'You don't know him,' I told Sukh, who touched his wound and begged to differ. I shook my head. 'No – that's just mild. Divy is dodgy – and I mean *dodgy*. He's into stuff . . .'

'What kind of stuff? Like he's some kind of bad man . . . ?'

'He's just a bit crazy. He's got all these dodgy mates and he's always hanging round with them . . . God knows what they do . . .'

'So you're saying he's some kind of *gangster*?' laughed Sukh.

'It ain't funny, Sukh. He's got all this money and not all of it comes from the family business. There's like this whole other side that—'

'Shit,' said Sukh, looking worried. Like he'd just remembered something that made him believe me. It turned out that he had. 'The first time I seen him,' he told me, 'there was this shit going on with some of my cousins and he got out of his car and Tej acted like he was scared of him. Or wary at least . . .'

'I've seen people do that when he's around,' I admitted.

'And you think . . . ?'

'I dunno what to think. I don't think he's a criminal or anything, but then I don't know where he gets his money – most of it. It's not all from the business . . .'

'But why would he go against your dad's word?'

'He wouldn't. He'd never let my dad agree in the first place. And he'll never forget . . .'

I'd managed to scare *myself*, never mind Sukh – and I was talking about my own *brother*. But I wasn't making it all up. Divy had always been a little bit scary. And now he was always dressed in leather, with a diamond-studded band holding his ponytail, and dripping in gold, going out at all hours and talking secretly into one of his three mobile phones. And if I *was* pregnant – well, there was no way he'd let that go. Not Divy. Suddenly I wanted to cry I was so scared.

'Look, he can't be all that bad, can he? If your dad—'

'Sukh, you're not *listening* to me,' I pleaded. 'You can't tell them – it'll make things ten times worse than they already are . . .'

'They couldn't get much worse, Rani.'

'Really? What do you think Divy will do if he finds out I'm—' I caught myself just in time. I was so angry and scared that I'd nearly told Sukh that I was pregnant – not that I even knew that I was . . .

Sukh raised an eyebrow again. 'That you're *what*?' he asked.

'Going out with you,' I said quickly, feeling a little sick.

I pulled further away from Sukh and stood up, hoping that it might help ease the nausea. All it did was make my head spin and then I felt the surge of bile and ran to the bathroom. Sukh followed me, once he'd realized what was happening, and held my hair as I threw up, using his free hand to rub my back.

Ordinarily I would have died of embarrassment but I didn't have time and Sukh's reaction to my apologies, after I had cleaned myself up, was to kiss me and give me a big hug. To tell me that it wasn't a problem. Just adding to the huge long list of reasons I had in my head that convinced me that I loved him more than anything in the world; that the two of us were born to be together. I could have kissed him until I died . . .

'I think you should call your doctor,' he told me still later, as we prepared to go back to our other lives.

'I think you might be right,' I answered, trying to hide my increasing fear.

'Maybe you've eaten something bad,' he suggested.

'Yeah, maybe,' I replied.

I looked at my watch and told Sukh that I had to go. He walked me down to the street and over to the taxi rank. Before I got into a car, he gave me a hug and told me not to worry.

'We don't have to tell them anything. We've got all the time in the world . . .' he said.

I couldn't reply. I couldn't say anything. I didn't know what to say. My legs were aching, my head spinning. We had all the time in the world. But the thing was that our world was about to come crashing down around us, like a furious waterfall, drowning us both . . .

 **RANI**

The following Saturday I managed to convince my dad that I needed to be at Natalie's house by eight in the morning. I told him that we were going to Alton Towers for the day with her mum, and perhaps because he was preoccupied by other things he didn't even give it a second thought, telling me to have a good time and giving me fifty quid. I packed a bag with a change of clothes and showered quickly before almost running to Nat's house in my Adidas sweat pants and T-shirt. I don't know why I packed the change of clothes. It wasn't like I was really planning on going to Alton Towers – or anywhere else. We were about to find out what was really up with me.

Nat was still in her pyjamas when she let me in, yawning and apologizing for looking like a gargoyle, which she didn't. I followed her upstairs, slumped down on her unmade bed and opened my bag. I showed her the box I had bought from Boots in town the day before and let her read the instructions. She didn't say a word as she opened the box and pulled out the information leaflet. Eventually she sat down next to me

225

and kissed me on the cheek.

'So when were you supposed to come on?' she asked in a sleepy voice.

'Nearly three weeks ago,' I said, not looking at her.

'And your boobs are swollen and you're being sick?'

'Yeah.'

Nat shrugged her shoulders and tried to smile. 'I think this is going to be a formality, baby.'

I looked at her. 'In what way?' I asked stupidly.

'Rani – you're pregnant . . .'

There was a knock at the door. Nat opened it and then asked me if it was OK to let Jasmine come in. I pushed the contents of the box underneath the covers and said yes.

Jasmine came and sat down on the bed, immaculately dressed in linen trousers and a white top, even at that time of morning. She took hold of my hand and smiled. 'I know, Rani,' she told me softly.

I glared up at Nat, who shrugged her shoulders before speaking. 'I'm sorry, babe. It's just that Jas knows what to do – she's got a friend who's been through it.'

'But I told you not to tell anyone,' I said, resigned to the fact that it made no difference if Jasmine was in on my secret or not. Either way, I was in big trouble.

'I'm sorry – I just wanted to get someone else's opinion,' Nat told me.

This time I shrugged my shoulders. I realized that Nat, despite her big-woman act, was just the same as me really. A teenager. Neither of us knew it all and if anything I was the one who was having to do the real growing up.

'I'm not going to tell anyone, Rani,' said Jasmine, squeezing my hand.

'I know . . . it's OK. Really.'

'Well then – we might as well get this over with,' said Jasmine, standing up.

Nat pulled the pregnancy test kit from under the covers and handed it to Jasmine, who read the instructions too. Then she turned to me and smiled kindly as my mind began to wander and I looked into her eyes, which were, depending on which day of the week you looked at them, either green, brown, grey or a combination of all three. I was trying to think of anything but the test. I would have given anything to wake up and find that this had all been a nightmare.

'And you haven't been for a wee this morning, right?'

'Yeah – Nat told me not to.'

'Good. Now here's what you have to do . . .'

As she explained, I sat there thinking about the last-cigarette cliché that I'd seen in so many films where someone was about to be executed, and wondered if you could smoke one in two minutes. Not that I'd ever been near one. Jasmine was talking about blue lines appearing or not appearing on the strip after the two minutes were over but I wasn't really listening. I was over by the window by then, looking out into Nat's mum's garden, with its hanging baskets, ivy and a blaze of summer flowers, thinking about Sukh and Divy and my dad. Wondering what I was going to do. My life had been like a wonderful pathway, with flowers and trees lining it. I had been walking it hand in hand with Sukh and Natalie and . . . and now I had reached a dead end and there was nothing that I could see to get me through. No way around the barrier to continue walking along the path. Doors were closing one by one, slamming shut on all my options, all my dreams.

I tuned back into reality, took the kit from Jasmine and went to the bathroom. I left the door unlocked and carried out the test, starting the timer on my mobile and waiting for two minutes. I sat on the loo looking at the seconds ticking away, edging me towards my fate. There were thirty seconds to go when I ran back into Nat's room, in tears. I got into her bed, pulling the covers around me, even though it was a hot and humid day. Nat asked me if I wanted her to check the strip for me and I nodded my head. She got up and went to get it.

On her return she showed the test to Jasmine, who looked at it, shrugged and then came over and kissed me on the forehead. She didn't have to tell me that it was positive. I already knew that it would be. I wasn't stupid – just scared and unwilling to let the truth intrude on my life. Jasmine stroked my hair and then looked at Nat, who came over and got into the bed next to me.

'We could sort out an appointment for you at a

clinic,' said Jasmine. 'D'you want me to get the info for you or even give them a call?'

I didn't reply. I just lay there and hugged myself, nodding through the flood of tears.

'It'll be OK, Rani,' Nat told me, putting her arms around me too. 'I promise. I'll look after you . . .'

Jasmine kissed me on the cheek, stroked my forehead and stood up. 'I won't be long,' she said. 'I'll have to pop back to mine and then I can get something sorted out.'

'OK,' replied Nat.

'Shall I tell Mum?' asked Jasmine, looking at her sister.

'What does it matter?' I croaked through tears.

She leaned in and kissed me again and then walked out of the room. I turned to face Nat and spoke through my tears once more.

'I'm going to get killed,' I told her.

'Ssh, Rani. No one's going to kill you. They'll have to kill me first.'

'You don't understand . . .' I wailed, but she just shushed me again.

'Let them try,' she replied.

I spent the rest of the day there, throwing up four times and trying to decide what I was going to do. When I was going to tell Sukh. *If* I was going to tell him. In the end Natalie persuaded me to wait until I felt stronger. I rang my dad and told him that I was going to stay at Natalie's for the night —we had got back late and I was tired. He spoke to Nat's mum and then told me that it was all right, that he'd speak to me in the morning. He sounded as though he was pissed off but I was past caring at that point. If my staying at Nat's upset him, then he was in for a major shock soon enough anyway.

Sukh sent me five text messages and tried to call me throughout the day but I wasn't ready to talk to him. Wasn't ready to tell him that we were in serious trouble. I thought about that path again, the one I had been walking down, and I wanted to pretend that I was still on it, still happy and carefree for just a while longer . . . And I thought about babies and Sukh and life without my family and all kinds of things until I fell asleep, holding onto Nat like she was a life raft in the middle of a stormy sea.

RANI

I rang Sukh three days later.

'Hey—'

'Why haven't you been taking my calls?'

His tone was flat and emotionless. He was angry and concerned at the same time. But his reaction was exactly what I'd expected. I mean, I had ignored him. What else was I going to get? He was hardly likely to bend over backwards to be nice. I explained that I was feeling sick and that I'd spent the past few days in bed, hardly eating or sleeping at all.

'You've still got that bug?' he asked in a softer tone.

'Er . . . yeah, something like that.'

'Something like *what*?'

'Don't be like that,' I told him, trying to summon up courage that I didn't have.

'Rani – what's going on?'

'We need to talk. Today.'

There was a pause for about thirty seconds before he spoke. I didn't interrupt the silence.

'Is there something wrong . . . ?' he asked, his voice quiet.

I knew what was going on in his head. He thought that I was angry. That I was about to dump him. In my mind I could see the hurt look on his face and I wished that I could hold him and kiss him. Tell him that I wasn't about to drop him; that I was actually about to turn his whole life upside down. And I didn't want to. I really didn't want to . . .

'No . . . yes. Look there's something wrong but it's not what you think, all right?'

'Then what is it?' he asked, sounding worried.

'I just need to see you. Can we meet in town?'

'Yeah . . . about midday?'

'Where?'

'At Parvy's. She's here but I think she's at work—'

'What's she doing in Leicester? I thought that . . .?'

'She's back here for a month – mainly for a holiday. That's what I was trying to call you about.'

'Oh . . .'

'She's helping at the office in Birmingham. I think she said she'd be back at three.'

'Well, shall we make it eleven then?'

There was another, shorter, pause. 'Whatever,' he replied, sounding pissed off.

'See you there.'

I rang off, lay back on my bed and burst into tears.

Divy pulled up at some traffic lights on London Road and turned to me. 'Why you always in town?' he said, looking mildly suspicious.

'What's it got to do with you?' I said, wishing that he would just shut up until he'd dropped me off.

'You want lifts here and there you better believe it's my business. I ain't havin' no one tell me that my sister is wandering the streets like some dutty white girl.'

I gave him a filthy look. His 'dirty white girl' reference was about Natalie and we both knew it.

'Well . . . ?' he demanded.

'I'm going to town to buy some stuff,' I said, knowing exactly how to stop his interrogation. 'Girl stuff.'

He pulled away from the lights, flying through a rapidly shrinking gap between a bus and another car. I held onto the dashboard and swore at him. He looked at me and grinned before jumping another set of lights, blowing his horn at a couple of students who he nearly ran over, and then pulling up opposite the railway station.

'Is this all right for you?' he asked, turning up the bhangra music that I had made him turn down earlier.

'Yes – I would say thank you but I can't be bothered.'

'You just watch yourself, Rani. I'm around town today. Best not get up to anything . . .'

My reply was lost in the slamming of the passenger door and the screech of tyres as he sped away. I looked at my phone, which I'd turned to vibrate only. Sukh had been calling me since ten and I didn't want to speak to him before we were tucked away from the rest of the world. He'd only ask me what I wanted to talk about and he'd know about that soon enough.

I walked down to Granby Street, ignoring a couple of tramps, and turned left into Belvoir Street, making my way round to King Street. Divy's car was parked up ahead of me outside a bar, his stereo at full blast. He was standing by the door with an Asian bloke who looked like a bouncer. He had a skinhead, barrel chest, huge arms and skinny legs. He was wearing a leather coat too, and around his neck was a thick gold chain that looked more like a rope. I wondered what they were doing outside a bar that early in the morning and why it needed a bouncer during the day. As I passed Divy grinned at me and told me to watch myself again. I flipped a finger at him and went on my way, praying that Sukh wasn't about to walk up behind me or call out to me from across the street. I didn't relax until I had reached New Walk, halfway to Parvy's building.

I checked my phone – it was only a quarter to eleven. I decided that I didn't want to be early and walked back down King Street, crossed the road onto Market Street and found a coffee shop. I walked in and ordered a drink. I sat in the window, going over and over what I wanted to say, not noticing the people wandering by like I normally did. I was losing my will, sitting there, thinking about the appointment I had for the following day at a clinic for pregnant girls. I was pregnant. I was actually pregnant. There was this thing growing inside me every day. A human being. Two men came in and sat a few seats down from me. One of them turned and smiled at me.

'Cheer up, love—' he began.

'Oh, stick it up your arse!' I shouted, for no reason whatsoever.

Then, turning red, I grabbed my stuff and hurried out, leaving the poor man sitting with a shocked look on his face. I ran back down the street towards Parvy's building, not stopping until I was outside. I dried my eyes and looked at my phone again. It turned eleven minutes past eleven as I looked at it. I pushed the buzzer and waited for Sukh to answer.

 **RANI**

I pushed the door to Parvy's flat open and walked in.
Sukh was standing at the entrance to the living
room.

'You didn't answer your mobile,' he said.

'I know – I was getting a lift in from Divy. I didn't
want him to know I was meeting anyone. Especially
not you . . .'

'Thing is . . .' began Sukh, nodding towards the
living room.

'What?'

'Are you going to invite her in or what, Sukhy?'
came Parvy's voice from inside.

I looked at Sukh and he shrugged. 'I was trying to
tell you . . .'

Part of me wanted to run out of the building and
back down the street. But where was I going to run to,
and what was I going to do when I got there? As much
as I wanted to put off telling Sukh about the baby, I
knew I couldn't. And once I had told him . . . Well,
Parvy knew everything else about us.

'Don't matter,' I reassured him.

'I thought you had something important to tell me,' he replied, looking confused.

I walked over to him and kissed him on the cheek. 'It's past the point where it matters if Parvy knows,' I said.

'Knows what?'

I walked past him into the living room and gave Parvy a hug.

'Hey, Rani, you look well,' she said, sitting back down on the sofa. She was wearing white trainers, flared jeans and a red top with white lilies printed on it. She looked great.

I smiled. 'There's something that I need to tell you both,' I said, feeling heat rising in my cheeks.

'What is it, Rani?' asked a confused-looking Parvy.

Sukh came and stood next to me, taking my hand. I started to cry.

'Hey . . . what's the matter?' he said softly, holding me awkwardly.

I pulled away and wiped my eyes. I had to say my piece. Had to get it out into the open . . .

'I've not been feeling well,' I began, noticing that I had Parvy's full attention. There was a question in her eyes.

I looked down at the floor. 'I've been sick and—'

'Did you go to the doctor's?' asked Sukh.

I put my arms around him and let the tears fall freely. 'I'm so sorry . . .'

He looked down at me and smiled. 'Sorry for what,

beautiful? You haven't done anything wrong.'

Parvy got up and looked at her brother. 'Do you want me to go out for a bit?' she asked, looking concerned.

'No – stay . . .' I replied.

'What's wrong?'

I pulled away from Sukh and managed to find the sofa through my tears. I blinked and looked at Sukh's face – so confused and hurt and worried. I was about to turn his life upside down and . . .

'I'm pregnant,' I told them, before putting my head in my hands and really breaking down.

Sukh came over and sat down, putting his arms around me and pulling me to him. He didn't say a word. He just held me until I'd cried myself dry. Parvy was standing by the window, looking out into the street, silent. I was still sobbing when she spoke.

'I thought you used—'

'We *did*,' said Sukh.

I looked at his face. It was ashen. I looked at Parvy. She was furious – I could see it in her face, even though, on the outside, she seemed calm.

'We must have split one—' I said.

'Or decided that you didn't have one handy but what the hell – one time couldn't hurt . . .' snapped Parvy.

'No . . .' I whispered.

'You're sixteen fucking years old,' she said, looking more at Sukh than at me.

'You're out of order, Parv – there's no need to swear at us,' Sukh snapped back.

Parvy thought about what he had said for a moment and then her face relaxed. She sighed and sat down on the floor in front of me and Sukh. She looked into my eyes as she spoke. 'You know that this is going to be bad, don't you?' she asked.

I nodded.

'Not just the pregnancy thing but the whole family bullshit too.'

I nodded again.

'And you're sure . . . ?' she continued.

Sukh looked at me. Tried to smile but failed. He swallowed hard.

'I didn't come on and I was being sick all the time,' I explained.

'And you decided to get a test . . . ?' said Parvy.

'Yes. I did it at Nat's house – it was positive.'

Parvy considered my words for a moment and then looked at me again. 'Have you arranged to see someone?'

'Jasmine – Nat's sister – sorted out something for tomorrow,' I told her.

'Is it a proper counselling service – a balanced one? Some of them are run by religious nutters . . .'

I hadn't even thought about an abortion until then. It was something that I'd always said I would never do. But I'd never been pregnant before and now I was. I didn't have a clue what I wanted to do. I was just scared.

'It's a women's advice service . . . Jasmine said they were really good to one of her friends when she . . .'

I started to cry again. Sukh hugged me close and told me it was all right.

'How can it be *all right*?' I asked through the tears.

'We're in this *together*, Rani,' he told me. '*Whatever* happens – it's you and me, OK?'

I held onto him like my life depended on it. He felt so warm and strong and safe. I just wanted to stay where I was and never go home again. Just be there, with him holding me, looking after me. But Parvy's words were going round in my head too. We were sixteen. How were we going to cope? What were we going to do for money? And more importantly, how were we going to stop our families from—?

Parvy stood up and paced the room for a few minutes. 'Look,' she said eventually, 'I'll give you whatever you need. Money – whatever. But this is going to be a difficult decision for both of you. You haven't got long to decide either. But if you decide that you are going to have a child then we have to tell Dad—'

'*No!*' I shouted. 'We *can't* . . .'

'Rani – if you *do* decide to keep the baby, how else can we deal with it? We're just going to have to ride the problems. Family feud or not, this is far too serious.'

'But my brother will kill me . . .' I pleaded.

'No,' replied Parvy firmly. 'No, he won't. This isn't the Punjab in the nineteen sixties. There are laws that protect you from your family.'

'He lays one finger on you—' began Sukh, with real menace in his voice, before Parvy cut him off.

'And that won't help either, Sukh. This is about stopping any violence – not starting more.'

'*Yeah?* I'm telling you *now*, Parv – he touches Rani and I'll kill him myself.'

'Forget it, Sukh. We're going to sort this out like normal people – not feuding farmers from the Punjab.'

'I'm not having an abortion,' I blurted out.

I don't know where it came from or why I said it but I did. I hadn't even considered the possibility and I wasn't thinking anywhere near straight. My mind was a rush of different thoughts and emotions.

Parvy looked at me and shrugged. 'What you decide is up to you, Rani, but have you thought about what having a baby at your age really *means*?'

I didn't reply.

'You've seen those girls in town, pushing prams and living dull lives,' she continued. 'Is that what you want?'

'Leave it, Parv,' said Sukh. 'It's not helping. We need to think about what *we're* going to do. This is as much my mess as it's Rani's.'

'What about college, uni? Don't you want a *career* first – a *life*?'

'*Parvy . . .*'

'All I'm saying, Sukh, is that you both need to think about this properly. Weigh up both sides. There's so much involved in having a baby. It's not easy—'

'If that's what it comes to – we'll deal with it,' replied

Sukh, holding me even tighter.

'Just think about what you're saying,' insisted Parvy. '*Really* think about it – and if you are going to have it – then, like I said before, we have to speak to Dad. You're going to need your family to support you – not least with Rani's family. God only knows how they'll react . . .'

The thing was, even then, I knew what they'd say, my family. What they would do. There was no way they would accept me and Sukh, never mind our child. What was I going to do? Parvy was right. If I had a baby, my life would change for ever. I'd have to leave home. And if Sukh's family didn't accept it, we would have to go it alone, no matter what Parvy did to help. And why would Sukh's dad be any different from mine when it came down to it? Even though he was calmer and more forward thinking, he wouldn't want his son's life ruined because of a baby. Not when his son didn't even know his GCSE results yet.

I was partly relieved that Sukh and Parvy knew. But only partly. It didn't change things – just made the load a little easier. Now I wasn't having to worry about telling Sukh. Now it was just a case of worrying about what we were going to do next . . .

 **RANI**

I took Natalie with me to the counselling meeting the next morning. Sukh offered to come but I told him that his being there would distract me. I'd be wondering what was going on in his head instead of thinking about what *I* wanted to do. I knew that it was his decision too, but first and foremost it was mine. He was wonderful about it. He didn't get upset or anything. Instead he told me that he would be on the end of a phone as soon as I was ready to talk and that he loved me and always would. He kept on saying that we would be fine — that we'd cope with whatever happened. And I was beginning to believe him too. He had this determined look in his eyes when he spoke about it — like he was ready to face up to any responsibilities that might come his way. If it had been the other way round I would have screamed at him, I think. I would have wanted to be part of everything. But he was really calm, although he admitted that he was really scared too, underneath it all. I suppose he was being strong for both of us — or trying, at least.

I had been so scared that his reaction would be

243

different – uncaring or unconcerned. In my head all these scenarios had played themselves out – he'd dump me, or tell me that it was *my* problem. He'd try to take over and make the decision for me and get all macho about it. But none of that happened. He just listened to me and comforted me and gave me all the love and support I needed. I mean, we were the same age and he was so manly about it, but in the best way. Really mature and open and honest. I'd never believed in soul mates until I met him, and now I was sure that was what we were. Soul mates. Destined to be together. It was the only way I could explain to myself how wonderful he was. I know it sounds silly and corny and all of those things but I really felt that way. He was like an angel. My angel.

By lunch time me and Natalie were walking through Victoria Park in the sunshine, avoiding games of cricket and football, stepping between the sun-bathers. It was hot and I was drinking from a bottle of water. The nausea had been better for a few days, just a morning thing rather than all day, and in my head I felt a little stronger, a little bit more in control. But the control was a fleeting thing because I knew that by the time I got home and was alone in my bedroom, the doubts would return. The worry and the fear too. But at that point I was doing fine.

We were discussing what the woman at the clinic had told me. How many weeks I had before I couldn't have an abortion. What social security I could claim.

Help with everything from nappies to dentists and doctors and all that stuff. She had also gone through a long list of hazards and pitfalls associated with giving birth and the aftermath, told me to consider whether I felt ready to be a mum. Was it something I could really see myself doing? She advised me not to discount the options out of hand but to think about them, talk things over with parents and friends. I didn't bother to fill her in on my family and the whole secrecy thing. I figured that she wouldn't have a clue about what to do, so why bother? It's not like there was a support group for girls who got pregnant by the son of their family's sworn enemy.

Nat was busy telling me to consider all my options. She had been pointing out that college would be difficult with a child in tow. Not to mention that I would never be able to go out or buy new clothes, never be able to be a teenager properly. I listened as she spoke, but there was something in me that was telling me to ignore what she was saying. I don't know where it came from, but a little voice in my head was telling me to have my baby. That was how I was thinking about it: not *a* baby but *my* baby.

'I'm having it,' I said defiantly. 'Right at this moment I feel like having it.'

Natalie sighed. 'Rani – have you thought about it . . . ?'

'*Thought* about it? That's all I have been doing. That and working out how not to get killed by my dad.'

'But it's a *baby*, baby. They cry and they poo and they puke all over the place.'

'Sounds a bit like me then—'

'Rani! It's not some toy that you can give back when you're bored.'

I looked at her and wondered if she thought I was being stupid. Then I realized that I was stupid for even questioning if Nat thought I was being silly. Of course she did.

'I know you don't agree with me but—'

'Look, you know that I love you and I'll be your friend no matter what happens – but I don't want you to regret this in two or three years' time when you're stuck with a kid instead of getting drunk at uni,' she said.

'I don't think I can do it anyway,' I told her.

'Do what?'

'*Have* an abortion.'

'Look – it's not the ideal solution, I know. *Ideally* you wouldn't be pregnant in the first place, but don't let that anti-abortion shit get to you. It's *your* body.'

'I know that – I just can't do it. I'd feel like I killed something . . .'

'Rani . . . you won't be killing anything. You'll be doing it in both your best interests – yours and Sukh's.'

'No, Nat. You don't get it. I don't feel right about the whole idea of having an abortion – I don't even know why—'

'You don't think that a woman should have the right

to *choose* . . . ?' She looked amazed and aghast at the same time.

'Don't be so stupid, Nat. Of course I agree with that. I just don't want it for myself. Why can't I disagree with abortion and still support someone else's right to have one. I'm not preaching to anyone else . . .'

'But—' began Nat, only for me to carry on.

'I just don't feel it's the right thing for me *personally*. Call it religious or cultural or whatever. I mean, I don't think abortion should be illegal or anything. I just don't agree with it for *me*.'

'Man, you think you know someone . . .' said Nat.

'It's still *me*,' I insisted.

'So you're not gonna start bombing abortion clinics or anything then?' she said with a smile.

'Nat – don't be an idiot. I'm not saying—'

'I know,' she said, interrupting me this time. 'I understand what you mean.'

'*And?*'

'*And* I think you're bonkers. But I'll still love you and . . .'

'What else?' I asked.

'If you *are* going to have a little monkey, can I be its godmother?' She had tears in her eyes as she spoke.

I smiled and gave my best friend a hug. 'Of course you can, Nat.'

'Can I buy it little trainers and stuff?'

'Yeah.'

Nat was off on one. 'I hope it's a girl – we can call

her Lily and buy her cute dresses and sing songs to her about fairies and princesses and—'

'Natalie?'

She looked at me with a grin. 'Yeah?'

'Can we leave all of this until after I break the news to Sukh?'

Her face fell a little. She nodded. 'Yeah I, er . . . for-got about him . . . You'd better speak to him first . . .'

I smiled at her although I was nervous again about Sukh's reaction. What if he wanted me to have an abortion? What if he didn't want to be a dad at his age? But then again, I didn't want to be a mum.

I just didn't have a choice in the matter.

Not a choice I could live with.

I rang him about an hour later. Nat and I had walked up to Allandale Road and I was sitting in a new bar. She had popped across the road to buy a novel from Browsers, our favourite bookshop, and I used the time she was away to make the call. He picked it up on the first ring.

'I'm keeping it,' I said before he had the chance to speak.

He was silent for a few moments and then he asked me if I was sure that I was doing the right thing. I was completely honest with him. I wasn't in the least bit sure it was the right thing according to every-one else, but it was the right thing for me. The only thing.

'Well, I guess that means *we're* keeping it,' he said, causing me to swallow hard to stop the tears.

'Yeah – I guess it does . . .' I said quietly.

'You mind if I tell Parvy?'

'Will she shout at me?' I asked.

'Maybe – but she'll help us, Rani – I know she will.'

'Yeah – tell her,' I replied. 'You know this is going to be hard, don't you?'

'Yes.'

'And you're sure you want to be part of it, Sukh?'

He waited just a beat before replying. 'Absolutely. You think I'm going to walk away from you now?' he said.

'I hope not,' I told him.

'I'd better start getting a plan of action together then . . .'

'We're gonna have to tell your parents, aren't we?' I said, resigned to it.

'It's going to be big steps all the way from here on in,' he replied. 'We may as well get the first one over with . . .'

I saw Nat come out of the shop. 'Nat's coming back so I'd better go. I love you, Mr Bains.'

'I love you too, beautiful. Call me later . . .'

'Try and stop me,' I said before ringing off.

As Nat came in and sat down I thought about what had just happened. I had just decided with my sixteen-year-old boyfriend that we were going to become parents. Just like that. It felt strange. Unreal. Like I was walking in someone else's dreamscape. But that feeling wasn't going to last much longer. I was going to be dragged back into reality soon enough.

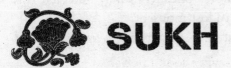 # SUKH

It took a week for Sukh and Rani to finally pluck up the courage to talk to Sukh's dad, a week of thinking and changing minds this way and that. Sukh was glad that he was finally about to tell him. He knew that there would be fireworks – he was ready for them – but he also had a feeling deep down that his dad wouldn't abandon him. He just hoped that he was right. The alternative – taking Rani and moving into his sister's flat, an option Parvy had already given him – would work but Sukh wanted his parents' backing. He didn't want to lie to them or break from his family.

He sat in the lounge, waiting for Parvy to arrive with Rani. They had agreed to let Sukh break the news and for Parvy to bring Rani to the house at a given time. It was a gamble, one that might backfire, but Sukh was ready for that too. In his head he was confident, strong, mature. In his heart he was all of those things but there was an extra emotion too. Fear. He tried not to show it as his parents walked in and sat down. Rani and Parvy were due any minute and Parvy was going to call Sukh on his mobile – just one ring to let him know that they were outside. Sukh had left his confession to the very last moment.

'What is this that is so important, *beteh*?' asked his dad.

'I've got something very serious to tell you,' Sukh replied.

'So serious that you invite your parents to a meeting at their own house and insist that they being there at set time?' continued his dad.

'Yes,' said Sukh, swallowing hard.

'Where is your sister, *beteh*?' asked Sukh's mum.

'She's on her way, Mum. She's bringing someone with her . . .'

'Who?' Sukh's mum's eyes bore into him.

'Someone . . .'

'What have you done, Sukhjit?' enquired his dad in a stern voice. 'If you've broken the law—'

'No, Dad – it's . . . Well, it's not as bad but it's maybe more serious,' he said, trying to find the right way to say his piece. The right words.

'I am not sure that I like this . . .' Resham Bains said to his wife in Punjabi.

Mrs Bains shrugged her shoulders. 'You remember we had this with Parvinder too,' she replied.

'Yes – "I am leaving home. I am going to America . . ." How could I forget it?'

'Then it will be the same thing,' reassured Sukh's mum, as Sukh's mobile rang to inform him that Parvy and Rani were coming up the drive.

'Mum. Dad. It's not like that – it's—'

'Spitting it out, Sukhjit,' urged his dad, almost beginning to grin at his son's hesitancy.

Sukh heard the front door open, heard footsteps approaching the living room. 'We're going to have a baby,' he blurted out quickly.

Resham Bains looked at his wife and then at his son. His mouth gaped. Sukh's mum raised her eyebrows, taking in the information slowly.

'*Who* is having a baby?' she demanded. '*Parvinder?*'

'No, Mum,' said Sukh, as the living-room door opened and Parvy brought a scared-looking Rani into the room.

Sukh's mum had to sit down quickly. Her hand went to her mouth.

Sukh looked at Rani and tried to raise a smile. He looked at his parents . . . 'Not Parvinder. *Us*. Me and Rani. Rani *Sandhu* . . .'

Sukh waited for the explosion. The backlash. The fireworks. His mum sat silently, her face drawn, as though she had seen a ghost. He looked at his dad. His dad's face was red. He stood up and began to walk slowly towards Rani, shock in his eyes. And then he began to cry.

He took hold of Rani, who was unsure of herself, looking at Sukh for support. Sukh put a hand on his father's arm but Resham Bains ignored it. He just stood and looked at Rani for what seemed like an age. Sukh's mind switched between relief and fear. He'd seen his dad cry twice in as many weeks, something he'd never experienced before. He wondered who would break the silence. It was his dad.

'Rani,' he whispered.

'*Sat Sri akal ji,*' replied Rani, saying hello in perfect Punjabi.

Sukh's dad blinked back tears. 'You look just like your aunt,' he told her.

Rani stood perfectly still. Sukh could see that she didn't know how to react. He took his dad's arm again. 'Dad – I think you should sit down,' he said softly.

'Yes, *beteh*,' replied his dad. 'I think you are right.'

He let go of Rani and sat down next to his wife. Parvy, who looked as shocked as everyone else, sat next to them. Sukh and Rani didn't move.

Sukh looked at his parents and lowered his head. 'I'm sorry,' he said, hoping that one of them would go mad and start to tell him off.

The situation was surreal. Sukh had expected an explosion and it hadn't happened. The fireworks had failed to light. He didn't know what else to do, so he took Rani's hand and told his parents everything. From the moment they had met through to Rani discovering that she was pregnant. He told them how Parvy had known about them, met Rani and told them both the story of the feud. He told them about Rani's dad and her brother, Divy. About being in love and being scared and not wanting to hurt anyone. And then he told them that he and Rani were scared of what would happen to them. Scared of what her family might do. It felt like he had been trapped in a box and had just been set free. He felt light, calm.

His mum spoke next. 'Do you know what you've done?' she asked in a hushed tone.

'Yes,' replied Sukh.

She looked at Rani. 'And you, Rani – you realize that there is no going back from here?'

'*Hanj-ji*,' agreed Rani in Punjabi.

'*Hai Rabbah!*' called out Sukh's mum suddenly. 'What *kismet* is this that you have given us?'

'Enough!' shouted Sukh's dad, making Parvy and Rani jump.

'I'm sorry, Dad,' said Sukh, thinking that his dad was about to get angry too and trying to defuse his rage.

'You are an idiot,' Resham Bains told his son in Punjabi.

'It's not all his fault,' said Rani, surprising Sukh with the force of her tone.

Sukh's dad looked at Rani.

'Please don't be angry with him alone,' continued Rani in Punjabi. 'We are both to blame. But how can we change what is done?'

'If it hadn't happened in the first place—' said Sukh's mum.

'It *has* happened,' said his dad.

'There will be more blood spilled over this,' continued Sukh's mum.

'*No!*' spat Resham Bains. 'We are not in a village in

the Punjab. We are British now and this will *not* destroy us. I will not lose a son where I also lost a brother . . .'

'But what can we do to stop the dishonour felt by Mohinder Sandhu?' asked Mrs Bains.

'You leave that to me, woman . . .' replied Resham Bains, looking at Rani.

Sukh took Rani's hand again. She hadn't moved from the spot. 'Rani, sit down,' he told her, only for her to shake her head.

'It's OK. I'll stand,' she replied.

'You know,' said Resham in Punjabi, 'I have thought about your father every day since my brother was killed. Every day. At first I wanted to kill him with my bare hands, to tear out his heart. But that didn't last very long. In time I realized that I had not lost one brother that day but two. Your father was my first friend. My childhood companion. We spent every day of our first fifteen years together. I miss him as much as I miss Billah and Kulwant . . .' He swallowed hard to hold back his emotions.

'I hope that this will bring our families together, child, not tear them apart as before – I will try to make sure of it. But if I cannot then I will accept you into my house, no matter what wrong you and my son have done. I will love you as my own daughter. If your father disowns you I will cherish you and help you to bring up my grandchild . . .'

Sukh watched as Rani's eyes streamed with tears and his dad went to her, hugging her tightly and stroking her hair. He heard Rani whisper, 'Thank you,' over and over again; watched until he had to hide his face to wipe away tears of his own. Resham let go of Rani and wiped his eyes before he spoke.

'For now this will go no further,' he told everyone in the room. 'Tomorrow I will pay a visit to Gianni Balwant Singh and ask his advice. He was a school-friend of ours, Mohinder and I, and he knows the family history. I will use him as a go-between and talk to Rani's father. There has been enough blood spilled over the years. Now we share blood and we will use that to end this feud. Perhaps the child these children have created will be the blessing that brings us back together . . .'

Sukh looked at Rani, wondering what she was thinking, what she was feeling. He hoped that his dad would be proved right. That he could really end the feud. He didn't want to have to face Divy Sandhu if it could be avoided. But something in the back of his mind told him that he might have to. Divy might never let go of the feud, just as Rani had said. He was still thinking about it when his parents went out to the kitchen to make tea. Parvy followed them. He turned to Rani and edged her towards a seat.

'Are you OK, babe?' he asked in a whisper.

'I'm just a bit shocked,' she replied. 'I wasn't expect-ing him to react like that.'

'I know,' Sukh told her.

'It's good, though – he could have thrown us both

out or just got really angry,' she said.

'It feels a bit like a dream though,' admitted Sukh.

'Well, it won't when my dad finds out . . .'

'What do you think to the chances of him being OK about all of this?'

Sukh saw Rani hesitate. Saw her eyes cloud over with fear.

'I'm praying that he'll be OK once the shock wears off,' she replied, 'but I'm not sure that he will be.'

Sukh squeezed her hand and then put an arm around her shoulders. 'We're gonna be OK,' he told her. 'I promise.'

'I do feel a bit better about it. You and Parvy were right about your dad . . . he's such a lovely man . . .'

'I just can't believe how he reacted,' Sukh said again. 'It was just the last thing I thought he would do . . .'

'Mine would have killed us both – talking of which, I'd better get going.'

'Come on, I'll walk you back some of the way.'

As they walked through the tree-lined streets of Oadby, wary of being seen by Rani's family, watching out for them, Sukh hoped against hope that Rani would be wrong about her father. For the first time since he had found out about the baby, Sukh felt a little more secure, a little more hopeful about the future and what it held in store. He looked at his beautiful girl-friend and realized that he was going to be with her for ever. They were going to have a child. He shuddered a little at the thought of it all, but only a little. He would be a dad by the time he was seventeen; have a child with the girl of his dreams. The whole thing should have made him run for his life. His friends would have, but he wasn't like his friends. He realized that the thought of bringing up a child with Rani actually made him happy. Happier than he had ever been in his entire life.

 **DIVY**

Divy pulled to a stop fifty metres away from them, the engine of his Audi humming in neutral. He looked again to make sure that his eyes hadn't played a trick on him. They hadn't. Fifty metres up Manor Road, and moving slowly away from him, was his sister, walking down the road with a boy like she didn't have a care in the world. He'd heard a rumour that his sister was knocking about with some lad but Divy had refused to believe it – until he saw it for himself. He thought about all her trips into town, staying over at that *goreeh* slag's house.

'Bitch.' He said it out loud, his face set in a grimace. There he was, respected all over town, and his fucking sister was laughing at him. The number of times he had warned her . . .

'Well, you get well and truly catch now,' he said, looking at himself in the rearview mirror.

Tempted to drive straight up and confront her, Divy fought to stay calm and decided to follow them. He slid the car into first and then second, cruising slowly. The CD player pumped out bhangra R & B fusion. Too loud, thought Divy. They'd hear the thump of the bass bins. He turned it off.

At thirty metres from the couple he took a right into a private road that ran up to a new estate of houses, built on land reclaimed from the university. The road ran round to the left, shielding him from their view, and bought him out at a roundabout on Stoughton Road. He was in front of them now. He pulled up again and waited.

It would take them five minutes to walk past him if they chose to take Stoughton Road. They might walk across and down the Manor Road extension. In which case he would be able to catch up with them by driving down the road ahead, which connected the two. She was obviously on her way home and there were only two or three ways she could go. With whoever the dead man was that she had with her. Divy wound the window down in a smooth electric whirr and spat. He waited.

Five minutes later there was still no sign of his sister. He pulled off again, across the mini roundabout and down Woodfield Road, reaching the end quickly. He stopped at the junction. He couldn't see them.

'Shit!' he said in a panic, hoping that he hadn't lost them.

He punched the dash, cutting a dent with one of his gold rings. 'Bastard!'

He looked up. There they were. They stopped to kiss and the blood in Divy's head began to boil. He wanted

261

to get out of his car there and then, but again he tried to stay calm and reversed along the kerb about thirty metres so that he wouldn't be seen. As he stopped he saw them walking on, heading down Launde Road. The boy looked familiar, but Divy was too far away to make out his face clearly enough. There was something about him though . . .

Divy waited again, two minutes this time, before moving forward and taking a right at the junction. He drove like a pensioner on a Sunday morning down Launde Road, edging forwards rather than moving. He saw them turn into Uplands. Left. He pulled up to a stop. He knew that his sister would take a right, past their uncle's house, along and then round onto Harborough Road at the top, not five minutes' walk from the house. Thinking about it, he realized that she would ditch the boy before she walked down Brookside, not wanting to risk being seen by Uncle Sohan. He sped down the remaining stretch to the junction and waited yet again. No sign of them . . .

He took a left and approached the corner with Brookside. Ahead, walking round the tight turn in Uplands, heading for the pub and the shops, he saw a lad. Probably the same one, but then again . . .

Ignoring the pair of legs walking away he turned right, and sure enough, walking slowly down towards Prince Drive, he saw his sister. He drove slowly after her, pulling up just past her as she walked up the incline. As she saw him, her face at first dropped and then changed quickly to a sly smile. Stupid girl . . .

The driver's window whirred down.

'Gonna give me a lift home?' his sister asked, smiling.

'GET IN!'

Rani jumped.

'Don't even come with the innocent shit . . . I saw you with some boy.'

She looked shocked. 'It's not what—' she began.

'GET IN! Before I run you down, you stupid little bitch . . .'

Divy watched his sister's face fall as she walked round to the front passenger side door. She opened it.

'In the back,' he spat. 'I don't want your dirty little mouth anywhere near me . . .'

Rani shut the door and opened the one at the back, getting in silently, her face red with embarrassment and fear. Mostly fear.

 **RANI**

'GET LOST!'
    I was sitting in the living room with Divy standing over me, shouting at me like the Neanderthal wanker that he was. My dad was in the room too, along with Gurdip. My mum had been banished to the kitchen. My heart was in my mouth and I was feeling sick. I was in big trouble. I couldn't believe that Divy had seen me with Sukh. We were both on such a high after meeting his dad that we had taken a risk. When Divy had pulled up in his bhangra-mobile I'd nearly fainted. My only saving grace was that he had no idea who the boy was. I shuddered when I realized what would have happened had he recognized Sukh. My life was turning into a nightmare before my eyes . . .

    'Who is he?' asked my dad, calmer than my brothers.
    'No one – just a friend from school.'
    'You think that I am the stupid, Rani?' said my dad. 'School bloody finish—'
    'He's just a lad that I know,' I insisted.
    Divy looked like he was about to explode. 'I ain't takin' that,' he spat. 'Who is he?'

264

'If you think I'm telling you . . .' I replied, trying to sound calm and unflustered. Inside I was more scared than I had ever been. Scared of my own family and what they might do.

'Well – if you don't then you're gonna be stuck in here . . .' Divy told me.

'You can't make me do anything,' I said. Suddenly I forgot to be calm and burst into tears.

'Cry all you like, Rani. You ain't going out nowhere from now on – believe me . . .' continued Divy.

'This is a *free country*!' I shouted. 'How you gonna stop me?'

'Think what you like, you *slag*!'

I looked at my dad, pleading with him with my eyes. He caught my gaze and looked away. His face was drawn and almost white. Like someone had ripped the life out of him.

'*Dad* . . .' I cried, trying to think of a way out. Something to get me away from my brothers and out of the house.

'When I asked you before,' he said in Punjabi, 'when I told you what would happen if I ever caught you with a boy, you looked at me with the face of an angel and swore that you were not one of those girls. Why have you done this to me, Rani? Didn't I look after you, give you everything . . . ?'

'*Dad!*' I screamed at him.

'Shut up! *Khungeri!*'

'I'm not a whore!'

'Then what are you? You have shamed me . . . cut off my nose,' he continued in Punjabi.

'Tell us who the boy is,' said Divy, 'and we'll let you off—'

'NO!' I screamed.

My stomach was turning over and over. My head was spinning and my throat was dry, like it had been sandpapered on the inside. I wanted to throw up.

'OK – have it your way, Rani,' Divy told me. 'From now on you ain't leaving the house. No phone calls, no town, no nuttin', innit. You don't speak to me or Dad and you definitely ain't speaking to the *goreeh* friend of yours. I bet she's the one put you up to this . . .'

'You can't . . .' I said in a whisper, feeling the bile work its way up my foodpipe.

'Yeah – we can. No college either. Nothing . . . You think I'm gonna let you make people laugh at me? At this family?'

I looked at my dad, who shrugged.

'Don't look at me,' he said. 'You did this, Rani. Not me. I don't have daughter now. Your brothers will decide what happens to you. Do not ask me . . .'

He walked to the drinks cabinet in the corner and poured himself a whisky, drinking it down in one and pouring another.

Divy sneered at me and grabbed me by the arm. '*Get to your room!*' he snarled, pulling me roughly from my seat.

I screamed and shouted and kicked at him before the

bile got too much and I threw up down myself. Divy looked at me with disgust and then laughed. Suddenly his hand shot out and he slapped me across my face, knocking me to the floor. Instinctively, my hands covered my stomach, protecting my baby.

I screamed again and shouted for my dad but he ignored my pleas, and between them Divy and Gurdip – who had spoken to me only once since I had arrived home, telling me that I was dead to him – dragged me to my room. As they pulled me up the stairs, I caught sight of my mum, tears in her eyes, her face set in the same expression as my dad's earlier. A cross between shock, anger and despair. As if their fate had poisoned them. I called to her but she scuttled back into the kitchen. I struggled to protect my belly as Divy and Gurdip threw me onto my bed.

'You don't come out until you reach marriage age *or* you tell me who that fucking bastard is – whichever comes first!' said Divy.

He walked out and slammed the door so hard that the frame split. For a few moments I lay on my bed, scared that they might have damaged my unborn child, before desperation took over. I looked around, frantically searching for my mobile. But it was in my bag and my bag was downstairs. I got up and wiped puke from my mouth. My face was stinging and my left eye was closing up. I walked to the bedroom door and opened it. Gurdip was standing in the hallway. He glared at me and left me in no doubt that I was going nowhere. I shut the door and returned to my bed, holding my stomach, the tears spilling down my face . . .

Later I was woken by the sound of a drill. I opened my eyes and saw my father holding my door open, his foot behind it as Gurdip fitted a lock. On the outside. I jumped off my bed and ran to the door.

'What are you doing?'

'What's it look like?' said Gurdip, forgetting his vow not to speak to me ever again.

'You can't do—'

'*Shut up!*' shouted my dad, giving me a death stare.

'I'll call the police!' I shouted back. 'This ain't the Punjab!'

My dad turned suddenly and raised a hand, ready to hit me. I shielded my face with my arms but there was no need. He looked at me and then turned his head away, dropping his hand.

'You call this love?' I asked him.

'This is for your own protection . . .' he said softly.

'Protection from what – *you*?'

I could see that words hurt him. He looked away again and told Gurdip to hurry up.

'You call yourselves my *family*? *I hate you! I fucking hate you!*'

I was expecting a slap but all I got was a baleful stare as I returned, beaten, to my bed. I slumped on it and started to cry again. My dad just looked at me. I spat out the rest of my words.

268

'You won't ever see me when I get out of here,' I told him. 'You've already lost a sister, now you're gonna lose a daughter too . . .'

His face twitched at the mention of his sister and he hurried out of the room, maybe shamed, maybe saddened. I didn't know, and I didn't care. Gurdip finished fitting the bolt and closed the door, leaving the wood shavings and dust on the carpet and locking me in. I thought about all those stories I'd heard about girls being kept prisoner by their families. I never thought that my family would ever stoop so low, take things to such an extreme. I was in shock, I think, trying to take in all the things that had happened to turn my world to hell. I sat there and wondered what I was going to do. How was I supposed to get out of there? How was I supposed to get back to Sukh?

I woke again around nine p.m., going into my en suite bathroom to shower off all the tears and the vomit. In the mirror I saw the bruise down the left side of my face. I saw it out of my right eye because the left one was closed over. I looked like I had run into a wall. I got undressed and turned the shower on, wondering if Sukh or Natalie had tried to call or text me. I was sure they had and realized that they would be worried when I didn't reply. I was hoping that one of them would figure out that something was up before my brothers searched through my phone for Sukh's number. I swallowed hard at the thought of Divy calling Sukh . . .

After my shower I gingerly put antiseptic cream on my bruise, right above my eye where Divy's hand had split the skin. The stinging sensation coupled with the sharp smell of the cream nearly made me throw up again. But I held it back and returned to my room. I sat at my desk, facing the bed. I had one of those swivel chairs and I span round on it, coming to a stop facing the screen of my computer. I cursed myself and my own stupidity. The computer . . .

I saw that Divy had removed the phone from my room – the land line – but he hadn't bothered to disconnect the modem of my PC. I doubted whether he even knew what the Internet was. I wondered if anyone was on the phone before realizing that if I logged on and someone tried to make a call, they'd realize that I was up to something. Instead I went to the door and listened as hard as I could. There was some noise from downstairs, the TV being the loudest. Probably Gurdip watching football or some other crap. My mum was usually in bed by ten and my dad rarely used the phone. Gurdip was the only one who might discover what I was doing. I looked at my clock. It was 9.45. I decided to give him another hour, lying back down on my bed and switching my TV on.

At ten minutes past ten I turned off my television and listened at the door again. The TV was still on downstairs and there were loud voices, maybe Gurdip and Divy. Maybe even my dad and some of his friends. I looked at the clock, decided that I couldn't afford to take a risk and settled back down to watch the telly. My intention was to e-mail Nat, who checked her e-mails every day, once in the morning and once at night. I'd probably missed her for the night but there was always the morning. I blinked at the TV, not really watching the late-night film that was on. I was busy concocting my future in my head, with Sukh and our baby. And waiting to get on line.

I finally connected at just past midnight, figuring that if anyone called now it was likely to be for Gurdip, in which case they would probably ring his mobile so as not to wake up my parents. I listened to the computer connect and then went to the door to check for noise. The house was silent. Gurdip was probably out with Divy or in bed. I went back to the screen and logged on to Hotmail. Deleting all the spam, I hit the compose tab and typed in Nat's address.

> Divy caught me with Sukh. Doesn't know who he is though. They've locked me in my room. Please tell Sukh and get him to call the police. I'm scared . . .

I signed it and hit the SEND button.

THE NEXT DAY

# RESHAM

R esham Bains hadn't slept a wink and the morning brought only fear and anxiety. And dreams of
old. He had set off from his home at eight that morning, taking a long walk over to Clarendon Park to find
Gianni Balwant Singh-ji, and his mind had been taken
up with thoughts of Mohinder Sandhu.

As he walked, the sun began to warm his bones. He
remembered herding water buffalo and drinking *lassi*
from metal cups that set his teeth on edge. Watching
Kulwant Sandhu as she swayed along the dusty tracks
that ran to and from the village, her forehead gently
perspiring in the unforgiving glare of the Punjabi sun.
The tall tales of witches and ghosts and snakes, as long
as the Great Trunk Road and as black as night.
Mohinder, chewing on a blade of grass as the two of
them crouched by the side of a rice paddy, watching
adulterous neighbours frolic. Carrying kindling home
for the evening fires and listening to the old women
chatter as they churned out one *roti* after another, and
the insects buzzed around the oil lamps.

He remembered too the way Mohinder had looked

into his eyes on the night that Billah had met his *kismet*. It had been a look of pity, of hurt, and most of all a look of grief, fuelled, he was sure, by the realization that their childhood had been a mirage, one that had disappeared that night, overtaken by hatred and loathing. He had long waited for a chance to repair the wounds, to reach out to his best friend, whom he had never forgotten, with a hand of peace and healing and redemption.

As he strode purposefully into the *gurudwara* and asked for the Gianni-ji, Resham prayed that he would be right. That Mohinder would see this second twist of fate as a chance to put the years of hurt and pain behind them. Yet part of him was ready to accept the worst. There was no guarantee that Rani's father would be willing to listen to his words of diplomacy. Hence Resham's desire to involve Balwant Singh, a respected elder in the community and a man of great wisdom and compassion.

The Gianni welcomed Resham into an office and offered him tea. 'It is a fine day to take a walk to the *gurudwara*,' he said with a huge benevolent smile.

'Yes,' replied Resham, wondering how to break his news.

'Is there some purpose for your visit this morning or are you merely here to give thanks?' asked Balwant Singh, sensing the weight on Resham Bains's shoulders.

'What can I tell you, Gianni-ji?' began Resham, his eyes beginning to water.

'Come, come, brother – what is it that makes your heart so sad in the house of our Teacher?'

'Gianni-ji, my *kismet* has conspired to put me in a very difficult position . . .'

The priest looked at his friend and sighed. 'It seems to me that such pain can only come from a loved one . . .' he replied, waiting for Resham to compose himself.

Resham took a sip of the spicy tea he had been given and remembered his brother Billah's face at the moment his life had been taken from him. He steadied himself emotionally. 'Gianni-ji, it is my son. My youngest – Sukhjit . . .'

As Resham's tale unfolded the priest sat back and listened. As was his way, he offered no interruptions, no judgements, allowing Resham to take his time and let the words ease his burden slightly. The tea was cold by the time the story had been told. The priest waited for a few minutes before speaking.

'This is indeed a grave matter,' he conceded.

'I need your guidance, Gianni-ji. Your advice,' replied Resham.

'Your proposal is backed by sound intentions, brother, yet I am unsure whether Mohinder will see it so.'

'Then you do not think that I should tell him?'

The priest shook his head. 'No, Resham, tell him you must. It is the only thing to do—'

'Regardless of his reaction?'

'Yes. I remember only too well the fate of your brother and Mohinder's sister. It is not something I wish to see repeated. I do not wish to see members of our community in jail or in a grave over such nonsense as honour and pride. It is not the way of the Sikh.'

'Yet if I *do* tell him, there is every chance that his rage will lead to bloodshed . . .' pleaded Resham.

The priest looked at Resham with a calming look on his face. He sighed and pushed aside a piece of paper on the desk in front of him. 'I cannot let it come to that. I will go with you to talk to your old friend.'

'When?' asked Resham.

The priest picked up the piece of paper and looked at it, thinking for a moment. 'Today – if we can. What is the point of putting it off? If we do not plant the fields today, Resham, we will still have to do so tomorrow . . .'

'Thank you, Gianni-ji,' replied Resham, the relief evident on his face.

'No thanks are required, Resham. It is my duty to try and bring your families together – if only for the sake of those two children. No matter what wrong our hearts tell us they have done – it is not for us to judge them. That is the preserve of our Lord . . .'

'Even though they have offended our ways . . . ?' asked Resham.

The priest sighed again. 'Perhaps we have never tried to find out what their ways are, my brother. The young people of today are not like us. Perhaps they have different values – who are we to judge? Perhaps the best thing we can do is try to understand . . .'

Resham looked at the priest with a combination of shock and respect. He wondered whether Mohinder could be as empathetic. As forgiving. He would soon find out, he told himself. It was up to the Lord now . . .

NATALIE & SUKH

'You're nuts, Natalie – you know that?'

Sukh shook his head as Natalie smiled at him.

'We should have just called the police . . .'

'We will . . . I just want to see if I can talk them round first.'

Sukh looked at her. '*Talk them round?* They've got Rani locked in a bloody room and you want to *talk* to 'em? Man, you're off your head . . .'

'We've just seen Gurdip being picked up by Divy. That only leaves her mum and dad . . .'

'Oh well, that's all right then – that'll make it a piece of cake . . .'

'*Faith*, fair Sukh. *Faith.*'

Natalie adjusted her hair, looking in a compact mirror before putting it back into her handbag. She had picked up Sukh after reading Rani's e-mail and driven him, in her mum's car – illegally – to within five hundred metres of Rani's house. They were waiting round a corner, ducking when they saw Divy's car leave.

280

Sukh sighed. 'We're gonna get caught, you know. I mean, you can't even drive—'

'I got us here, didn't I, sweets?'

'But you ain't even got a licence,' Sukh reminded her.

'It's an *automatic*, Sukh. How *hard* can it possibly be? I mean, I know driving is supposed to be this great coming-of-age malarkey, but *please* . . .'

'What about your mum?'

'She's away for the week – what she don't know—'

'Nuts . . .' said Sukh, more to himself.

'Yeah – something you are obviously lacking . . .' said Natalie.

Sukh ignored her and looked at his mobile. It was 11 a.m. and they had been sitting there for two hours watching the driveway to Rani's house. He looked at what Natalie was wearing and decided that he had to be as crazy as she was. He would have called the police himself otherwise.

'So, why are you wearing that suit? You look like a trainee accountant or something.'

'It's Jasmine's,' replied Natalie. 'The glasses too. They're not real. Got clear lenses in them . . .'

'And the point of the suit, the glasses and that clipboard is *what* exactly?'

'And the *hair*,' smiled Natalie. 'Don't forget the hair. It took me ages to get it into a bun.'

'Nat . . .'

'It's a little disguise,' she told him.

'But you look just like you, maybe a little older . . .' Sukh pointed out.

'Yeah, perhaps. But the last time I saw Rani's dad he was too busy looking at my legs to notice my face.'

'But he'll never go for you as—'

'*I wonder, Mr Sandhu, could I have a moment . . . ?*' answered Natalie in a very refined accent that was deeper than her real voice.

'Bloody hell!' said Sukh, genuinely surprised. 'You sound like a politician . . .'

'*See?*' smiled Natalie, returning to her own accent. 'Most people will fall for an official-sounding voice, a clipboard *and*—'

'*And what?*' asked Sukh, clenching and unclenching his toes to get the blood flowing.

'– a phone call,' finished Natalie, taking her mobile out of her bag.

Sukh watched in silence as she dialled a number, told him to shush, and waited for an answer.

'*Ah, good morning. Is that Mr Sandhu – Mr Mohinder Sandhu?*'

He heard a faint answer.

'*My name is PC Condew. I'm with the community policing unit . . .*'

Sukh was about to say something but stopped short when he heard Natalie repeating herself.

'*Yes, that's right . . . Police . . . I'm doing house calls this morning, looking at security in the home . . . Yes, that's right.*'

I have to visit every house on the street and this morning it's your turn . . .'

Sukh heard Rani's dad's voice, but again only faintly.

'On the contrary, Mr Sandhu, your English is more than adequate . . . Yes, this morning. I'm afraid it's compulsory . . . You have to receive my visit . . . Yes . . . Yes, well actually I'm round the corner with my fellow officer PC Nutless . . . No, no, no . . . just me. He is visiting another house . . . It won't take ten minutes of your time . . . Yes . . . Oh, in about five minutes? Excellent . . . See you then. Good morning . . .'

Natalie snapped the phone shut.

'You're off your bloody head!'

'Leave it out, Sukh . . . Just listen to me. I'm going in now. Wait here until I give you a call – I'll leave the front door open for you . . . If I call it means that I've got them out in the garden and the coast is clear. Then you grab Rani and get her into the car—'

'Are you absolutely—?'

'Just shut up and listen, will you? You're *such* a drip sometimes . . . All you do is wait for my call. You go in, up the stairs and round to the left. There's two doors at the end of the corridor. The last one is Rani's bedroom. Round to the left—'

'Right . . .'

'No, you spoon – *left* . . .'

'Right, that's what I said . . . left,' replied Sukh.

Natalie groaned. 'Jesus, what is this – a *sitcom*? Just go left, OK?'

'And if the coast *isn't* clear or you get caught out . . . ?'

'Then we'll call the real police.'

'But why can't we just call them now?'

Natalie gave Sukh a filthy stare. '*Whose* girlfriend is being kept prisoner . . . ?' she reminded him.

Sukh thought about Rani and Divy and everything else. He forgot his concerns about Nat's plan and nodded his head slowly. 'OK,' he said. 'I'm cool . . .'

'We'll see about that soon enough,' said Natalie.

She grabbed the clipboard and handbag and got out of the car, straightening her business suit out and heading for the driveway. Sukh watched as she approached the door and knocked on it, pulling out a card of some sort when a man opened the door. Rani's dad. She asked him some questions and then walked with him to the side of the house, where a gate opened out to the back of the house. Sukh watched as Rani's dad forgot to close the front door, his attention firmly focused on Natalie, who was pointing at something, playing her role. She might be nuts, Sukh thought to himself, but she was brave with it. And then he lost sight of her.

 **DIVY**

Divy Sandhu sat in the office of the family's hosiery unit and fumed. He had to think of a way to get his sister to tell him the name of the boy he had seen her kissing. Even the thought of it made him angry. The insult to his name. The damage to his family's respect. He turned the situation over and over in his mind . . . There had to be a way of getting her to tell. There *had* to be. As he sat and thought, Gurdip walked in and set a mug of coffee down on the table for him.

'How we gonna get her to tell us who the bastard is?' Divy asked his brother.

Gurdip thought about it for a moment and then shrugged. 'Dunno, bro. I reckon she'll tell us soon enough.'

'She ain't told us so far . . .'

'Yeah, well, she's still playing the big woman, innit. See how quick she is to deny it all after a week of being locked in . . .'

'Yeah, but will she *tell* us?'

Gurdip shrugged again. 'We could slap it out of her,' he offered.

285

'What good is that gonna do? Besides, she didn't say nothing yesterday when I slapped her . . .'

'Maybe Mum can get her to talk?'

Divy considered the idea of letting their mum sweet talk her but then discounted it. He wasn't about to let his mum feel even more shame than she already did.

'Hey,' laughed Gurdip, 'you taken to carryin' hand-bags, bro?'

Divy wondered what he was on about. For a second maybe. The handbag . . .

He grabbed it from the desk and rummaged around in it.

'What you doin'?' asked Gurdip, wondering whether the pressure was getting to his brother.

'I brought it with me because,' he replied, as he looked through it, 'she might try to use this . . .' He pulled out her mobile phone and smiled.

'What about it?' asked Gurdip.

Divy sighed at his brother's stupidity. 'If she's been messin' about with some lad,' he said patiently, 'then she's been callin' him, innit? Which means the number has to be on this . . .'

He looked at the screen. The battery level was low and there was a red warning light flashing. No problem though. The phone was the same make as his own. He pointed to his charger, sitting on top of a low filing cabinet. 'Pass me that thing there,' he said.

Gurdip picked up the charger and handed it to Divy. Divy took it and plugged one end into the wall socket behind his desk and the other into the [...] and the battery meter showed that it was [...] found the phone book and scrolled throug[h...] few minutes he showed the screen to Gur[...] numbers,' he said. 'I looked in the DIALLED NU[...] menu and she's been calling these two number[...] most. One says "SKH–M" and the other one's "SK[...] H" . . .'

'Mobile and home, innit,' smiled Gurdip. 'But what does SKH mean?'

'It's his name,' replied Divy, his stomach turning slightly as a thought entered his brain. He stared at the screen. 'It's Sukh,' he told his brother. 'Has to be.'

'Sukh? Sukh who?'

Divy felt a tingling around his hairline. His pulse speeded up. *If that's who I think it is* . . . His rage struggled to contain itself inside him. He scrolled to 'SKH–H' and pressed the green DIAL button.

Someone answered on the fourth ring.

'*Yeah – this phone I'm using was lost at football,*' began Divy. '*It looks like it belongs to Sukh but I don't know which Sukh, innit* . . . *Yeah, at the football match* . . . *Sukh Bains* . . . *Cool – I know him* . . . *Yeah, I'm a mate* . . . *Oh yeah, I'll make sure he gets it* . . . *Later* . . .'

He rang off and looked at Gurdip, whose eyes were about to pop out of his head.

'That number whose I think it is?' said Gurdip.

'Yeah,' replied Divy with an edge of steel to his voice and fury in his eyes.

He lit a cigarette and stood up, picking up his car keys. 'Come on – I need to pick up a couple of the lads and then you and me are going to talk to our slag of a sister,' he said.

'And then what . . . ?' asked Gurdip.

'*Then* we're gonna go see Mr Bains, man . . .'

The intent in Divy's voice was unmistakable. He looked at his brother, his eyes on fire.

Gurdip felt a rush of fear. Something bad was about to happen.

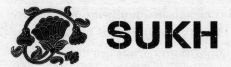 # SUKH

Sukh's phone rang about ten minutes after he had watched Natalie disappear into the Sandhus' garden. He answered it on the second ring, his nerves jangling.

'Yeah . . . ?'

'The spider has caught the flies . . .'

'Huh?'

'The spider— Oh, for God's sake . . .'

'Oh, right.'

He rang off and got out of the car, looking around to see if anyone was watching. Happy that he was not in any danger he ran towards the front door. He waited for a second or two before going in and then headed straight up the stairs, taking them two at a time. At the top they led round to the left and the right. Sukh went left and down the corridor. The first of the doors he came to he ignored. The next one had a lock on it, a bolt. It had to be the right one.

He threw the bolt and opened the door with a knock. When no one answered he pushed the door further open. Rani was lying asleep on her bed, her face swollen down one side and one of her eyes closed over. Sukh felt his fists clench involuntarily and he saw red. He wished that Rani's brothers and her dad were there – so that he could batter them for hurting her. Breathing sharply to catch himself and calm down, he walked over to Rani and shook her awake, covering her mouth as she woke.

Rani wriggled underneath him as he smiled and then removed his hand.

'SUKH!'

'Come on – let's *go!*' he whispered excitedly.

'What . . . ?'

He pulled Rani from her bed and handed her the only clothes that he could see, a pair of jeans and sweatshirt. '*Quick!*'

'What are you doing?'

He gave her a kiss. 'Rescuing you. No time to explain . . . we have to go. *Now!*'

Rani hurriedly threw on some clothes and then grabbed a bag that sat by her bed. She ran to her bathroom and gathered some stuff. Then she opened her cupboards and stuffed in some more clothes and underwear. She turned to Sukh and grinned as widely as she could manage.

Sukh felt the anger rising in himself as he looked at her. 'What happened to your face?' he asked.

Rani shrugged and said she'd tell him later. She seemed to be in a daze.

'Come on . . .'

Sukh led Rani out of her bedroom and made sure that he locked the door behind them. They ran downstairs and out of the front door. Sukh had reached the car before he turned round to find Rani standing at the edge of the drive, staring up at the house. He ran back to her. 'Rani – we have to leave . . . *Come on!*'

He grabbed her hand and ignored her tears, pulling her to the car. They got in just as Natalie emerged from the Sandhus' house with Rani's father in tow. Sukh watched as she wrote something on a bit of paper and handed it to Mohinder Sandhu. Then she turned and walked briskly towards the car. Sukh opened the door as she approached.

Nat stared at Rani, crying in the back seat. '*Oh my God!* What the hell did they do?'

'*Later*, Nat!' shouted Sukh, his adrenaline pumping. 'We have to get going . . .'

Nat briefly touched Rani's hand and then she turned and started her mum's car, pulling away at speed.

 # DIVY

Divy lurched his car into fifth gear as he sped along St Saviour's Road, narrowly avoiding an on-coming bus.

'SLOW DOWN!' shouted Gurdip.

'Relax . . .' said Divy, his mind racing. He wanted to get home fast and confront his sister.

In the back seat Johnny Sangha, a barrel-chested doorman, held onto the leather seats for his life.

At the top of St Saviour's Divy turned right onto the ring road, flying up the hill past the entrance to the General Hospital and down past Crown Hills School. He jumped the lights at the bottom and sped up Wakerley, headed back to Oadby. He only slowed down once he had reached Gartree Road, spotting a police speed trap at the roundabout. He eased down and proceeded at a snail's pace until the police were out of sight. At the junction that led back into Oadby he turned right, put his foot down and bounced across two mini roundabouts, reaching the lights of Stoughton Road and the A6 in record time. He took a left and headed for his dad's house.

'You're crazy, bro . . .' said Johnny, pretending that he was unfazed by the breakneck speed at which Divy had been driving.

'Shut up and listen,' spat Divy. 'We pick up the old man and then we're going to get that Bains dog . . .'

'Cool,' replied Johnny. 'No need to get funny wit' me, man.'

'I'm payin' you a grand for this, you get me?' snapped back Divy. 'I'll get funny wit' anyone I like.'

Johnny shut up and checked his pocket, where a brass knuckleduster nestled, waiting for an outing.

Divy turned into his dad's road and came to a stop on the driveway of the house. He switched off the engine and jumped out of the car, almost running to the door and opening it. Gurdip came after him, telling Johnny to sit and wait. Gurdip caught up with his brother in the living room, as Divy explained what he had found out about Rani's mystery boyfriend. At the mention of the name Bains, Mohinder Sandhu turned pale.

'Well?' asked Divy in Punjabi. 'We going to talk to her . . . ?'

Mohinder Sandhu mumbled something about fate and God.

Divy looked at him with disgust. '*Kismet?* Forget that, Dad. This is about pride. Our pride.'

'Nah, Divinder,' said his dad. 'This is too far . . . leave her alone. I will speak to this boy's father myself.'

Divy's mother, who had remained silent, spoke up.

'What are you saying?' she asked her husband.

'Keep out of it!' he snapped in reply.

'What is this?' she continued. 'Are we to be the victims of that family again . . . ?'

'I said to leave it—' shouted Divy's dad.

'Will no one avenge our child?' spat Divy's mother, ignoring her husband.

'Mum's right,' agreed Divy. 'This is the last straw . . .'

He turned and walked out of the room and up the stairs. Reaching Rani's room, he slid the bolt back and opened the door. The room was a mess and there was no sign of his sister. His rage flipped into overdrive as he returned, swearing, to the living room.

'*Where is she?*' he demanded.

His parents looked at him as though he had gone mad.

'Where's who?' asked his mum.

'Rani . . .'

'She is upstairs, my son – in her bedroom.'

A creeping realization dawned across his mother's face. She put her hands to her head and cried out. 'The *police*!'

Divy shot his dad a look. 'What's she talking about?' he asked. 'What police?'

Mohinder Sandhu stood up and pulled a card from his back pocket, handing it to Divy. 'They came this morning,' he said, a man in shock, with resignation written across his features and tears in his eyes.

'*PC Condew and PC Nutless* – is this some kind of

joke?' Divy replied, throwing the card to the floor.

'You what?' asked Gurdip, wondering what the hell was going on.

'It wasn't the police,' said Divy, ready to explode but fighting it as much as he could.

'*Hai Rabbah!*' cried his mother, calling out to God.

'PC Condew conned us!' added Divy. He looked at his dad with no emotion except pity. 'Is it up to me to keep this family's name from the mud?' he asked him.

Mohinder Sandhu said nothing.

'Are you coming or not?' asked his son.

'Yes . . .' whispered Mohinder, his mind full of a dark day, years earlier.

'Good.'

'But not to fight, Divinder. It is my place as your father to sort out this mess—'

'Do what you like, old man!' spat Divy. 'But that Bains boy is mine . . .'

He turned and headed out of the door, not caring whether anyone followed him or not.

 **RANI**

We drove the short distance to Sukh's house and Natalie dropped us off, promising that she would return later in the day, once she had returned the car and got changed into normal clothes. I gave her a big hug and kissed her about ten times, thanking her over and over. I felt so relieved. She left after making me promise to call the police and tell them about the way Divy had assaulted me. I told her that I would and kissed her again.

'Easy, babe,' she smiled. 'Sukh might get his panties in a twist if you carry on like this.'

'I love you,' I told her, kissing her again.

'Enough—'

'I do . . .'

Nat grinned at Sukh. 'You *lucky* boy,' she said, giving him a hug and a kiss.

'Thanks, Nat,' he replied, giving her a squeeze.

'Oh stop it, you two – you'll have me in tears.'

She got into her mum's car and drove off like a lunatic.

★ ★ ★

Inside, I let Parvy apply some more cream to my bruises. She asked me what I wanted to do and I told her that for the moment I was happy to let things go. But Parvy insisted that I at least let her take a photo of my injuries, just in case I wanted to tell the police later. I waited as she took out her digital camera and then snapped my face from about three different angles.

'I'll download these later,' she told me, giving me a hug.

Sukh's mum and his brother Ravinder were in the kitchen when Parvy brought me downstairs. I said hello to them both, politely in Punjabi, and then followed Parvy into the living room where Sukh was waiting. I felt a little embarrassed but at the same time I felt like I was safe too. The argument with my family had really scared me. And the way my dad had let Divy hit me, and done nothing about it. It was as though something had snapped between us. At that point I still didn't really understand it – the feeling was too fresh and too surreal. It would take a while until I felt normal again. A long while.

'Where's Dad?' Sukh asked Parvy, as we sat down.

'At the *gurudwara* – he's gone to see the Gianni.'

'Oh . . .'

'Should be back soon enough. He rang to tell Mum that he wants to take you with him to see Rani's father—'

'He *can't*!' I told them.

'It's OK, Rani,' replied Sukh. 'Once he sees what

297

they did to you he won't want to go anyway—'

'I don't want him to. Can't we just leave it? I can tell the police and maybe they'll stop my family from coming after me and . . .'

Sukh put his arm around me. 'Ssh . . . it's all right. Everything is all right. They won't ever touch you again . . . I promise . . .'

'Really . . .?'

He kissed me. 'Really. You and me are together now. For *good*. *Nobody* and *nothing* is ever going to change that . . .'

I pulled him close to me and listened to his heart-beat, took in his smell. I felt safe. Secure . . .

I woke up with a jolt to an argument going on outside. I couldn't hear what was being said or make out who was there, but there were raised voices and for a moment I thought that Sukh's family were arguing. Over me . . .

I got up, went to the window and looked out into the drive. I saw Parvy, Ravinder and Sukh arguing with three men. One of them was the bouncer I had seen Divy talking to outside the bar in town. The other two were my brothers. There were five or six other men there, neighbours maybe, and Divy was being held back by someone. Then the someone turned his face to the house and I saw who it was. *My dad*.

It took me a few seconds to register the scene before me. To check that I wasn't still asleep.

My heart jumped and my stomach knotted up. I ran to the hall and out into the driveway, screaming at them to go away.

Parvy saw me first and grabbed me, pulling me back towards the house. 'Come inside,' she told me sternly. 'I've called the police—'

'NO!' I shouted. 'I want them to leave!' I started to cry.

'It's OK, Rani – the police will be here any minute . . .'

I heard the sirens in the distance, wondering why the police were responding like they would to an emergency. Surely for a verbal dispute they wouldn't put on their—

Then Divy pulled free from my dad. I saw the flash of steel in his hands as he lunged at Sukh, his face contorted with rage. Everything felt as though it were slow motion, like time was tired . . .

Sukh jumped out of the way and Divy stumbled to the floor. I saw the bouncer pull something from his pocket and as two of the men I didn't recognize tried to block him, he smashed one of them in the face. The man cried out in pain and went down, blood spurting from a cut.

I screamed again and again. The sirens were closer now, maybe just round the corner . . .

Sukh kicked out at Divy as he tried to get up. The kick caught Divy in the mouth and he went down again . . . Then Gurdip kicked out at Sukh and caught him in the stomach. Sukh retched and went down on one knee, holding his middle . . .

I couldn't move. I was numb. I wanted to stop them but my legs were frozen and my mind was spinning.

One of the neighbours grabbed Gurdip and threw him to the ground, going down on a knee, holding him there. Divy got to his feet, wiping blood from his mouth. He screamed abuse at Sukh in English and Punjabi. Ravinder, Sukh's brother, tried to intervene. The blade swished through the air in a murderous arc and caught Ravinder on the arm, cutting through to the bone. Ravinder screamed and went down . . .

A police car screeched to a halt on the drive and two policemen jumped out. Another arrived, then another, followed by a van. The sirens wailed and flashed; tears blurred my vision.

Divy's friend, seeing the police, punched one of the neighbours and started to run. A policeman gave chase. I saw Divy lunge again, his arm out in front of him, the glint of sunlight on that cold blade . . .

I saw Sukh on the ground and forced my legs to work. I broke away from Parvy. The policemen were shouting at everyone to get on the floor. Divy was screaming abuse . . .

I ran to Sukh as my dad grabbed Divy. I helped Sukh up and held onto him for my life, sobbing un-controllably. My dad saw me. His hold on my brother loosened slightly. I held his eyes for a moment and then buried my face in Sukh's shoulder, happy that the police had arrived.

My dad called out to me. His words seemed slurred and distant. I made out my name – he called me his little girl, pleaded with me to go to him. Sukh had his back to the scene and held me tightly. I screamed, 'NO!' and looked into Sukh's eyes, seeking out his strength.

 **RESHAM**

Gianni Balwant Singh and Resham Bains pulled to a stop outside Asda on the A6, letting the police cars pass them, lights flashing, on their way to some crime scene or other. Resham mumbled something about the world in which they lived and then returned to staring out of the window of the priest's Ford Fiesta, as they moved off once more. They had talked at great length about what they were going to do and the priest had decided that the boy, Sukhjit, was man enough to accompany them when they went to meet Mohinder Sandhu. After all, he had reasoned, the boy had been man enough to father a child.

More police cars sped by in the outside lane of the dual carriageway. Then a van.

'There must be something very serious up ahead,' remarked the priest.

'Yes,' agreed Resham Bains.

'Perhaps someone's fate has conspired against them today,' added the priest.

'It is the will of our Lord,' replied Resham.

'Only His . . .' confirmed the priest.

* * *

They pulled up behind a police van outside Resham Bains's home. The priest turned to say something to Resham but spoke to an empty passenger seat. Resham had left the car almost before it had come to a halt and was making his way slowly towards the aftermath of an altercation. The Gianni-ji noticed that Resham's shoulders had sagged and that his legs nearly buckled.

'Lord, what fate is this that you have put before me?' he asked in a whisper.

Resham Bains walked slowly towards the people that he loved. He caught a glimpse of his wife and daughter, crying. He saw the policemen holding onto members of the Sandhu clan, talking into radios. Lights were flashing and sirens wailed . . .

Resham made his way to his son, kneeling before him. He saw blood seeping from a wound, discolouring the driveway. Gently, he touched his face. His son opened his eyes and tried to speak but the words failed . . .

'Ssh . . . do not try to speak, Ravinder,' he told him.

He stood up, looking to find his other son. He saw Sukh holding onto Rani, relieved that his youngest was fine. He saw Mohinder Sandhu, standing two metres from the lovers, holding onto Divy, tears in his eyes, his face racked with pain. Resham started to speak, to say something to his old friend—

* * *

303

And then Resham watched Divy break free from Mohinder and lunge at his youngest son . . .

Frozen to the spot, Resham saw the flash of steel and heard the cry of rage as Divy pushed the blade in with all his strength . . .

He blinked. Saw his son stagger, still holding onto Rani, and then fall to the floor.

He blinked again, saw the police spray something into Divy's eyes, smelled the pepper. He turned and saw his old friend once more. Mohinder said something . . .

Resham looked back to his son, heard women screaming, watched blood pooling on the ground underneath his boy. Memory played a cruel trick and flashed Billah before his eyes . . .

Resham fell to his knees, broken beyond repair. He cried out to the Heavens . . .

 **RANI**

I never saw it coming. Didn't realize until it was too late . . .

Sukh smiled weakly, kissed my forehead and told me he would love me for ever. Then something changed in his eyes. A light began to sparkle in the pools of soft amber honey and then it seemed to just dance away . . .

NEW YORK
TWO YEARS LATER

She crossed the intersection of West Broadway and Murray Street, ignoring the 'DON'T WALK' sign flashing at her. Her mind was elsewhere, filled with images of blood and memories of screams . . . A taxi driver shouted at her as she walked. She put his voice out of her mind. There was only one voice she wanted to hear . . .

The crossing at West Street flashed 'WALK' at her and she hurried across, heading down towards the Hudson River. Tears worked their way slowly down her cheeks and her heart pounded in her chest. Her honey-brown hair was piled on top of her head, and the combats and tight T-shirt she was wearing clung to her in the humidity of a New York summer. She brushed another tear away and walked on.

At the corner of New Murray and North End Avenue a hot-dog vendor tried to cheer her up by flipping forward and walking on his hands. 'Smile, lady,' he said to her, once he'd stood upright again, his accent a curious mixture of New Jersey and Ethiopia. She tried to smile at him but it didn't come. Just more tears . . .

Ahead of her, a group of tourists got off a bus fresh from JFK Airport and stood outside the Embassy Suites Hotel. She walked past them, wishing that *his* face would appear from amongst them. Knowing that it was never going to happen but wishing all the same . . .

Where North End Avenue met Vesey Street she stopped and, just for a moment or two, looked up at two memorials: the first to the great Irish Famine and the second to a much more recent tragedy. She looked down at the single rose she was carrying and wondered if it was enough of a memorial to her lost love. Whether *any* memorial was *ever* enough for people to forget that their love had been taken from them . . .

She found her way down to the Esplanade, a river walkway that ran down through Battery Park City to the park itself. Reaching the railings, she found a bench and sat down, placing the rose beside her. She looked out at the Hudson and wondered what *he* would have made of Manhattan.

Across the water she saw the Statue of Liberty looming through the slight mist just to the left of Ellis Island, and she wished that *he* were there too, sitting where she had placed the rose, talking excitedly about *their* holiday in Manhattan, taking a boat out to Liberty Island, or heading uptown to Central Park to laze around in the sunshine and eat hot dogs, maybe visit MOMA. She knew exactly what he would have said. How his face would have looked. She would never forget it. *He* was with her every day . . .

A boat sped past as she remembered. She thought about her mother and father. The brother − who had taken her life from her and thrown away his own. She thought about *his* father, sad and broken inside, with a sense of loss set in his eyes, as if for ever. How his mother longed . . .

She wiped more tears and stood up. She didn't want the thoughts she was having. Didn't want to mark the date with tears and bitterness and blame. She had done enough of that . . . It couldn't define her life for ever, the anger and pain. She refused to end up bitter, if only for the sake of—

Behind her she heard the sound of wheels clattering over paving. She walked to the railed edge and leaned over, holding the rose out in front of her. She looked up at the clouds and pictured his face. She whispered words of love and released the flower. A slight breeze caught it and it floated down into the water. She wiped another tear and said, 'I love you.'

'I thought you'd got lost, honey,' said a voice from behind her, in a fake New York accent.

She turned and smiled weakly at Natalie. But she couldn't reply. Natalie sensed this, let go of the pushchair and gave Rani a hug.

'I'm sorry . . . ' whispered Rani.

Natalie realized that her friend was talking to the rose, heading out into the unknown.

'Let's look at the river, baby,' she said, turning back

to the little boy in the pushchair.

The boy looked up at his godmother through amber-coloured eyes and grinned.

'Shall we take a walk down to the park?' said his mother.

'Yes,' replied Natalie, 'unless you'd like another few minutes . . .'

'No, it's OK,' replied Rani. 'Besides, I told Parvy we'd meet her outside Trinity Church in an hour.'

'Come on then, baby boy,' Natalie said to the toddler. 'Let's go see Aunt Parv . . .'

The boy gurgled with delight.

Also available from Bali Rai

(un)arranged marriage

Harry and Ranjit were waiting for me — waiting to take
me to Derby, to a wedding. My wedding.
A wedding that I hadn't asked for, that I didn't want.
To a girl who I didn't know . . .

Set partly in the UK and partly in the Punjab, this is
a bitingly perceptive and totally up-to-the-minute
look at one young man's fight to free himself from
family expectations and to be himself, free to dance
to his own tune.

0552 547344

The Crew

Mess with one of us — then you have to deal with us all

Billy, Jas, Della, Will and Ellie are the Crew.
And where they live — in the concrete heart of a big
city — you need a crew to back you up. Then one
day they find a fortune in notes and life becomes
very dangerous . . .

0552 547395

about the author

BALI RAI is still a writer from Leicester. If anyone asks, he is also still young and often exciting. Mostly he is too busy trying to get his next project in on time. As a Politics graduate, if he absolutely *had* to get a real job, he'd pick journalism. For now, he is happy to write, although he quite misses working behind a bar. However, this is more than made up for by the fact that he can now get out of bed when he likes and that nice people keep asking him to visit them in wonderful places all over Europe. Long may they continue to do so.

Rani & Sukh is his third novel for Corgi. The first, *(un)arranged marriage*, appeared on a number of award shortlists and won the Angus Book Award, the Leicestershire Children's Book Award and the Stockport Schools' Book Award. He was also threatened by an old Punjabi woman with what appeared to be a sandal. He thinks it may have been his mum but isn't too sure. Until he finds out he'll carry on writing his next story and try to stay out of sight.